The Purloined Corn Popper

By the Same Author

(THE McGURK MYSTERY SERIES)
The Case of the Wiggling Wig
The Case of the Absent Author
The Case of the Fantastic Footprints
The Case of the Desperate Drummer
The Case of the Weeping Witch

(OTHER BOOKS)
Hester Bidgood, Investigatrix of Evill Deedes
The Ghost Squad Breaks Through
Time Explorers, Inc.

A FELICITY SNELL MYSTERY

The Purloined Corn Popper

E. W. HILDICK

MARSHALL CAVENDISH   NEW YORK

Marshall Cavendish
99 White Plains Road
Tarrytown, New York 10951-9001

Library of Congress Cataloging-in-Publication Data
Hildick, E. W. (Edmund Wallace), date.
The purloined corn popper / E.W. Hildick.
p.   cm.
Summary: Ten-year-old Tim is worried when a popcorn popper containing a wad of
money is stolen from his kitchen and his friend Freddie is suspected of the crime.
ISBN 0-7614-5010-6
[1. Mystery and detective stories.] I. Title.
PZ7.H5463Pu 1997 [Fic]—dc21   96-51195 CIP AC

The text of this book is set in 12 point Sabon
Printed in the United States of America
First Edition

3 5 6 4 2

Contents

A Popper Called Hippo

Tim Kowalski was in deep trouble.

It happened one dull, rainy morning in the summer vacation. He'd been left to look after the house while his mother was at work. His best friend, Freddie Fisher, was with him. Both boys were crazy about video games. Tim had recently been given a new one called Power Patrol for his tenth birthday. They could hardly wait to start.

It was a game for two players. One had to drive a police car. The other, his partner, had control of the weapons: handguns, shotgun, and a deadly laser gun. It was up to him to choose which. He could also call in a helicopter backup team.

They had to chase a car full of bank robbers, who were shooting back. The police driver had to keep swerving to avoid being hit. The shooting partner had to keep trying to shoot the bandits first, without hitting innocent citizens. The boys played this all morning up in Tim's room.

Freddie was the better driver. Also the better shooter. This didn't worry Tim. Freddie was eleven. He'd had more practice. And Freddie Fisher was one of the best video games players in town.

But Tim was catching up.

And this was a great game.

Even Freddie the expert was impressed.

"Great game, Tim!" he said. "Especially the sound track." He turned up the volume.

The gunshots rang out louder than ever.

The screech of brakes sounded like cats fighting just outside.

And above all this was the wailing of sirens and the screams of pedestrians.

The noisiest of all was when the shooter called in for helicopter assistance. Then the CLATTER-CLATTER-CLATTER drowned out everything else.

Everything else except the mighty yell of "HOY!!!"

Something in that shout made Tim switch off the game.

"It's Mom!" he said, getting up. "Sounds mad."

He blinked in a shaft of sunlight. He hadn't even noticed when it had stopped raining.

The boys went downstairs.

Sure enough it was Mrs. Kowalski.

She was standing by the door that led straight into the kitchen.

She glared at Tim.

"Where is it?"

"Where—where's what, Mom?"

"Hippo," she said. "The corn popper."

Both boys turned to the counter. There was an empty space between the multispeed mixer and the microwave oven.

Even Freddie was looking puzzled.

Hippo was far too big to disappear without anyone noticing. The corn popper was more than fifteen inches high. It was made of light green plastic. It had a hippo head with a vast gaping mouth, two greedily popping eyes, and a red cap. It was made to look as if it were squatting. Like this:

The cap was removable. That was where you poured in the popping corn. The mouth was where the hot popcorn came out in a tumbling, gushing stream.

"Just like it was throwing up," Tim had said, soon after his mother had bought it.

She'd got it because she said it would be healthier than the oily kind. "Hot-air, low-cal."

But after Tim had said that about throwing up she hadn't seemed all that keen on it. Anyway, although it was rarely used nowadays, it was left to squat on the counter like some kind of kitchen god.

"It was there when I arrived," murmured Freddie.

Tim said nothing. His mother was still glaring.

"Well?" she said.

"It—it's gone . . ."

"You're darned right it's gone! Gone *where* is what *I'd* like to know!"

Tim shrugged. "How would *I* know?"

"Yes, how *would* you know?" said Mrs. Kowalski. "I suppose you've been upstairs fooling with that game all morning. Pushing buttons."

"Well—"

"I suppose it didn't occur to you to push the one button that matters!" she said. "The one on the doorknob. To make sure it was safely locked. Whoever snuck in didn't even have to pick the lock or break any glass. They simply walked straight in. Without wiping their feet."

"Huh?" grunted Tim.

"Muddy footprints! Look!" His mother pointed to a set on the tiled floor, fading as they got closer to the microwave corner.

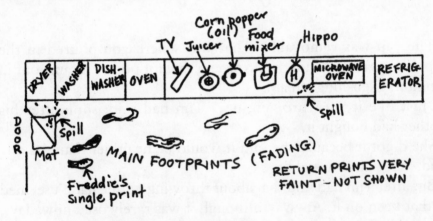

"Hey, yes!" Freddie started forward.

"Hold it!" Mrs. Kowalski held up a large hand, flat against his chest. "Isn't it time you went home for your lunch, Freddie Fisher?"

Freddie took the hint. "Yes, 'm," he muttered, stepping carefully around the first of the footprints.

Which left Tim to face his mother's anger all on his own.

2

The Clues

"Whoever left those prints sure knew what they were after," murmured Tim.

The footprints were large—adult size. There was also something very strange about them. What was it?

Then he realized. Most footprints showed the pattern of the soles. These were perfectly plain. Plain and flat.

"I'll clean them up, Mom."

"No! Leave them be! You'll destroy the evidence!"

"Evidence? You're not thinking of calling in the *police*? Just for the sake—"

Tim stopped. The doorbell. His mother opened the door.

"Oh, it's you again!" she growled.

Freddie was standing there, looking worried.

"Just one thing, ma'am."

"Yeah? What?"

"Why would anyone swipe a crummy corn popper when there's the food mixer next to it?" Freddie took a step forward, careful not to tread on the muddy prints already there, but leaving a new one of his own. "It must be worth four or five times as much as the popper."

Mrs. Kowalski glared at the new print.

Freddie's footprint   Intruder's footprint

"Maybe he likes popcorn," she said. "A real popcorn freak. Maybe he couldn't resist grabbing the popper."

"Oh . . . yeah!" murmured Freddie. Then he shook his head. "But didn't Hippo make only the hot-air kind?"

"Sure, but—"

"The nonoily kind?"

"So what?"

"So why didn't he swipe that regular oil model instead?" Freddie pointed to the dome-shaped appliance next to the juicer. "I mean, you never use Hippo much, do you, Mrs. Kowalski?"

Tim's mother blushed. She was very anxious about her weight.

"What difference does *that* make? The point is it's been stolen. Anyway, I thought you were going for your lunch."

"Sorry, ma'am. I just thought—"

"Yeah," said Mrs. Kowalski, opening the door and steering him out. "Thanks for your interest, Freddie."

When she'd shut the door she swung around to Tim.

"Now *he's* gone, I'll tell you why I'm reporting this to the police. That corn popper happens to be where I've been stashing the tips I work my fingers to the bone for down at the salon. I had a roll of two hundred and eighteen dollars stashed deep down in Hippo's heat chamber."

"Gee, Mom, I'm sorry! I had no idea. . . ."

"Of course you didn't! But now you know why I'm calling the cops, okay?"

"Yes, sure."

"Now that it's gone, corn popper and all—thanks to *you*—all I'm left with is a set of muddy footprints and . . . Huh! What's *this*?"

She peered down at the counter. Just in front of the microwave there was a small heap of brownish crystals. A *dash* really.

"It looks like sugar, Mom. The crunchy kind."

Tim wet a finger and reached forward. His mother smacked his hand away.

"Don't! It could be deadly poison!"

"It *does* look like brown sugar, Mom."

"I can see that. But what's it doing *here*? The only kind *we* use is the soft powdery stuff. Leave it for the cops to analyze."

She looked down at the floor.

"Hey, here's some more!"

Tim followed her. This spill was slightly smaller. Just a sprinkle down by the bottom of the door, but more widely scattered.

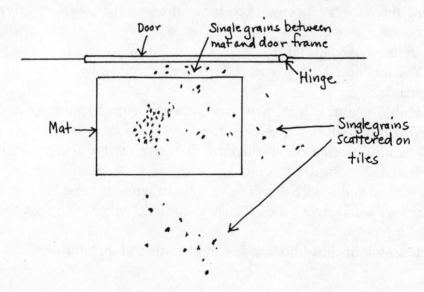

Armed with all this evidence, his mother called the police department.

Tim edged close enough to hear snatches of the conversation at the other end.

"A *corn popper*, ma'am?"

"Yes."

"Called—*Hippo*—did you say?"

"Yes. It was shaped like a hippopotamus. A green one, about one foot high."

Tim heard a guffaw in the background. Then:

"Yes, lady. I think I know the kind."

"But it wasn't *just* the popper," said Mrs. Kowalski. "I'd stashed over two hundred dollars inside it."

"Peculiar place, ma'am. How about if someone had switched the popper on?"

"Listen, officer, it's never used for popcorn these days. And now let's get serious. I'm reporting a *crime*."

"Sure, we'll look into it, ma'am. It's just that we have a backlog of intruder thefts. I've marked it for the attention of Detective Delaney."

"Detective Delaney?"

"Yes, ma'am. Don't worry. He'll be stopping by before the weekend."

"Huh!" grunted Mrs. Kowalski, after giving the address and hanging up. "Before the weekend, he says! And today's Tuesday!"

When his mother mentioned the detective's name a huge black shadow had crossed Tim's mind.

It was so sudden he didn't have time to wonder why. He knew there *was* a detective called Delaney, but he'd never even seen the guy. Strange!

He shook his head briskly. It would come to him later maybe.

Meanwhile, his mother was still looking miserable.

"Never mind, Mom. The insurance'll cover it."

"Insurance?" she snapped. "*What* insurance? Do you think— Why, yes!" she said softly. "Insurance. Thanks for reminding me. The Tim Kowalski Home Insurance Agency."

"Mom?"

"*They'll* pay. And the claim goes in right now. That's nineteen ninety-nine to replace the popper, plus the two hundred and eighteen dollars. Total: two hundred thirty-seven dollars and ninety-nine cents to be stopped from your allowance at the rate of five dollars a week. Just for starters!"

Tim swallowed hard.

It looked like his troubles were only just beginning!

3

Felicity Snell, Junior Librarian—and Private Detective?

"But *Mom*!"

It would take him *months* to pay off that amount!

But this *was* only for starters.

"Any other boys," his mother said, "they'd a been out in the yard, practicing basketball shots. Then nobody could have snuck in."

"But it was raining—"

"So if you'd been up in your room, *reading,* you'd have heard them."

"Reading?" yelped Tim. "That's *school* stuff, Mom!"

"But how could you hear anything for that game?" his mother continued. "Bang! Crack! Screech! . . . Anyway, you're playing no more video games for the rest of the vacation."

"But, *Mom*! What'll I do instead?"

"You'll go to the library right after lunch and you'll become a member. That's what!"

"Aw, Mom!" Tim was close to tears. But his mother's face was stony. She had to work very hard for her tips at the Cuts 'n' Curls hair-styling salon.

"Library," she repeated. "Right after lunch. You join." Then her face brightened. She'd just remembered one of the best tips she'd received in recent weeks. "Hey, the new librarian. Felicity Snell!"

"Who?"

"Ms. Felicity Snell. She used to be a private detective. Maybe she'll be able to give *you* tips. Advice on how to protect your property. Hey— and could be she'll give you advice on your own special problem."

"*Which* special problem?"

"How to find out who stole the popper and its contents. Then if we get them back, it won't have to come out of your allowance."

This time *Tim's* face began to brighten.

"But—who *says* she was a private detective?"

"She has her hair done at the salon. Everyone's been talking about how she once worked for a big nationwide outfit—Coast-to-Coast Investigations, Inc."

Tim's eyes narrowed. He was beginning to remember hearing rumors about the new librarian from some of the kids at school. Not being a regular library user, he hadn't paid much attention. *Now* it was different, though!

"Yeah, but was she any *good* at detective work?"

"Ha! *Felicity Snell?* Listen. Let me tell you just a few of the things we got to hear about her. . . ."

Mrs. Kowalski looked around and lowered her voice automatically, as if back at work exchanging hot gossip with a customer. Getting Tim to sit on a high stool, she took out the scissors and began fixing an unruly tuft of his hair.

"Sure," she said, "some of this is rumor." (Snip! Snip!) "But a lot of it's what Felicity herself told us. Backed up by what other customers have told us.

"Some of them knew her from when she was a kid here in West Milbury. She was always a book lover, they say. I guess that's why she got a good degree in English. With a librarian diploma, too. But her hobby, well, *one* of her hobbies—because she was very active in sports and outdoor stuff—well, her one deep-down hobby was playing at detectives.

"Some say she got the detective bug from Rick Delaney. *Keep still!* Same class. Tracing missing cats, dogs—that kinda thing. Him and a bunch of kids including Felicity."

"Uh—would this Rick Delaney be—?"

"Detective Delaney of the West Milbury P.D.? Yeah. *Just sit still, will you?* Detective Take-his-time Delaney who's supposed to be looking into our case. . . ."

"So how did Felicity Snell get to be a *real* detective? I mean if she trained as a librarian—?"

"Well, that's the kind of gal she is. She got herself a job as a librarian, sure. But a librarian *where?* With the big Coast-to-Coast private investigation firm, that's where. Seems they have their own library. Reference books on crime."

Mrs. Kowalski checked off the various subjects with a snip of the scissors for each.

- Fingerprints.
- Forgery.
- Alarm systems.
- Law books.
- Medical books relating to murder.
- Poisons.
- DNA testing.
- Fibers in evidence.
- Different kinds of dust, etc.
- Footprints—

"*What* prints?" Tim glanced down at the floor.

"Footprints. *But do keep still!* With books full of patterns of soles

18

and heels. Every boot and shoe ever made. Also patterns of tire tracks."

"Some library!"

"I'll say! And *that* ain't school stuff! That's detective *working* stuff! Inside a couple of years Felicity had gotten herself a transfer to what she called field operations. Undercover work mainly. She could turn her hand to so many things."

Tim listened, enraptured, as his mother went on to describe some of Felicity's undercover triumphs. Such as:

• Helping to resolve the Midwest Circus Wars, when she worked for a spell in one of those rival circuses, using her natural gifts for gymnastics and acrobatics, as a trainee trapeze artiste.

• Solving the Kentucky Derby Horse Doping Scandal, by working as a veterinarian's assistant, aided by her natural love of animals.

• Helping to bust the shopping mall Purse Snatcher Gang, by posing as a street entertainer.

"And that's just a few," said Mrs. Kowalski.

"But if she was all that good, why come back here to work as a junior librarian?"

"Nobody seems to know. Some say she had to shoot a man dead on one of these operations. Self-defense. And she had to quit to give herself a chance to recover. Others say there was some terrible crime being plotted—" Mrs. Kowalski dropped her voice— "concerning the West Milbury library . . . and Felicity had been sent to investigate. Posing as a librarian. What else?

"Then again others say she just got tired of all the heavy crime and came back for a rest."

Mrs. Kowalski gave Tim's hair a final snip. "Anyway, once you've become a library member you'll probably get to know more for yourself. As well as solve this mystery."

"I sure hope so!" murmured Tim.

He'd just remembered when he'd first heard about Detective Delaney. All of four years ago.

That had been the name of the officer who'd arrested Freddie's father for stealing from parked vehicles. Open and shut. Mr. Fisher had freely confessed to over one hundred similar offenses. He'd been jailed for three years. He'd been released about a year ago, but he'd never come back home. He'd gone off to live somewhere down south.

Freddie himself never spoke about this matter. But Tim knew how it had made his friend very uptight. Imagining people were always looking for signs to see if he was going to turn out like his father. Like father, like son.

And *that* was why Freddie had seemed so nervous. Scared of becoming the prime suspect. Freddie Fisher: present at the crime scene. Son of a convicted felon.

That was probably why he'd come back to point out that if *he'd* been the thief, he'd have swiped something more valuable.

Also that was probably why he'd planted his own muddy footprint right next to one of the thief's, to show how much smaller it was.

Freddie was certainly smart enough to think of that.

But would it work?

Tim sighed. He knew his mother didn't approve of Freddie. But that was because she blamed him for getting Tim involved in video games, not because of Freddie's father. Even so, she *had* looked a tad suspicious. . . .

"Hey, Mom," he said. "I hope you don't think—"

He broke off. He was going to ask if she really did have suspicions about Freddie. But just then the phone rang. Some customer asking if she could be fitted in for an appointment later that afternoon. Tim thought better of it. No point in directing his mother's attention even to the possibility of Freddie's being the thief. So he went up to his room to get ready for his visit to the library.

It seemed that if anyone could help them track down the real culprit, Felicity Snell could.

Tim could hardly wait now to see her!

4

"The Worst Detective in the World"

Five minutes later, Tim had just left the house when someone called out, "Hey! What's the hurry?"

Tim turned. It was John Farrell, a kid who lived opposite Tim's house. He was thirteen but looked older, tall for his age. Usually he ignored kids in the lower grades, even those who lived nearby. He always seemed too busy with crazy ideas of his own.

"You talking to me?" said Tim, wondering what made Farrell look so eager now.

"I hear you've been robbed," said the older boy.

Tim felt his heart sink.

That was *all* he needed!

J. G. Farrell sticking his nose in!

J. G. Farrell, full name John Gerrit Farrell.

"Who told *you*?" asked Tim.

"Never mind who told me," said J. G., looking snooty. He had that kind of face. His eyes were set deep. They were overshadowed with dark, down-sloping eyebrows that made him seem as if he was looking down his nose. His black hair was cut very short. This showed off his high, broad forehead. "A sign of brain power," he'd once explained to Tim's mother, when he'd asked her to style his hair like that. And, sure enough, those eyes and that forehead did give him a kind of all-seeing, all-knowing look. Especially the right eye, which was silvery gray—sharp, keen, penetrating. The left eye was a warm, rich brown and not at all sharp. Dreamy, in fact.

"*Have* you been robbed or haven't you?" he said, with an impatient glint in that right eye.

"Well—"

"Two thousand dollars, right?" The brown eye was beginning to glow. "Two thousand in used, unmarked bills. Stashed in a fireproof money box. In a secret hiding place. Inside the microwave oven. Snatched from under your nose. . . . That's the story, right?"

Typical! thought Tim. Trust J. G. Farrell to get hold of a rumor and blow it up into a full-length news report! Complete with times, dates, amounts, victims' statements. *And all of them wrong!*

No wonder some people said that J. G. stood for "Jump-the-Gun" Farrell. The kid who could make entire mountain ranges out of a couple of molehills.

Like the time a new family came to live in town. Kept themselves to themselves. Never chatted about where they'd come from. J. G. Farrell's verdict: "Fugitives. Wanted in twenty states." And when he found out the father had been hired by the local supermarket's meat department: "There! The guy's that mass murderer wanted up in Montana. Cuts his victims up into hundreds of pieces. But the FBI will be closing in, don't worry!"

It didn't matter who J. G.'s imagination got to work on. He'd even used it on himself. Starting from the fact that his father, mother, and four older sisters all had red hair while his alone was black. It didn't matter that his father and two of the girls had the same high foreheads and down-sloping eyebrows. It didn't matter that his mother said the black hair had skipped a generation or two and went back to her grandparents. It didn't matter that his father laughed it off by saying, "I guess you can't have all this fire without smoke!"

To J. G. it was proof that he'd been adopted. That his parents were so upset at having only female kids they'd adopted a boy to break the run. He'd figured it all out.

"My *real* mother," he'd said, "was an Arabian princess. My real father was a high-ranking American diplomat who managed to smuggle me out in the diplomatic baggage. If I told you his name you'd be surprised. Very, very surprised."

The only person to be surprised was J. G. himself, when Mr. Farrell got to hear of what he'd been saying and grounded him for one whole month.

Tim took a deep breath.

"Well, whoever told you this robbery story didn't have the facts right," he said. "Not by a *mile*."

J. G. didn't even blink.

"Maybe she didn't tell *you* all the facts. Maybe your mom was too shook up. Too mad. She *sounded* mad, over the phone. Even from where I was standing."

So that was it! thought Tim. His mom had been blabbing again. That call making a hair appointment must have been from Mrs. Farrell.

Then J. G. added something that stopped him in his tracks.

"If you ask me, kids like you, Tim Kowalski, ought to be careful who they let into their homes!"

"What—what's *that* supposed to mean?"

"I mean that I didn't see any strangers hanging around this morning," said J. G. "It sounds to me like an inside job."

Tim's heart sank even deeper. It looked like Freddie was being suspected already!

"I mean what else *could* it be?" J. G. went on. "A regular open-and-shut inside job. With an on-the-spot obvious perp with a family history of larceny." He pulled a card from his pocket and handed it to Tim. "Loosen up, kid. Your troubles are over. J. G. Farrell rides again!"

Tim stared at the card. Homemade. He'd seen it before. One of J. G.'s old hobbies.

J. G. FARRELL
THE KIDS' OWN DETECTIVE
NO CASE TOO BIG OR
SMALL

"I dug it out as soon as I heard. We'll soon have this little matter solved and the money restored. No problem."

Tim handed the card back.

"That's okay, J. G. Thanks, but no thanks. In fact, I'm just on my way to see a real detective."

The black eyebrows shot up farther.

"Oh yeah? Go ahead, if that's the way your mom wants to handle it, of course. They know all about the Fisher family down at the police department." He shook his head. "But they're slow. Slow, slow, slow! The jerk might have spent the money by the time *they* get around to it."

"I'm not going to the *police*," Tim said with a shudder. "I'm going to see what the new librarian—"

"Oh, *her*? Felicity Snell! You've got some hopes! What makes you think she'll be interested in an open-and-shut case like yours?"

Just jealousy, Tim decided. Anyway, he wasn't for hanging around and arguing.

He hurried on his way.

With this new threat hanging over Freddie, Tim was now more anxious than ever to get to the library. Because this *was* a threat.

As far as he could remember, J. G. Farrell, the Kids' Own Detective, wasn't just bad.

Bad detectives are poor at solving mysteries—sure. But there are some bad detectives who're not only hopeless at finding out who committed a crime, they jump the gun. They accuse the wrong people. They even scratch around for evidence to support their mistake. Sometimes they even *manufacture* such evidence.

Those are the worst detectives.

And Jump-the-Gun Farrell was one of these.

In fact, J. G. Farrell was probably the Worst Detective in the World!

5

More About Felicity

The Fisher house was on the way to the library. It came at the end of a street of mean little single-story houses. The yard was cluttered with junk—broken toys and furniture, an upturned barbecue grill, and old garbage bags filled with dead leaves.

Tim stopped by. Freddie was emptying a mess of charred food into the garbage can. Tim could see the blue haze still drifting from the open kitchen door.

"I *told* you it was burning, Freddie Fisher!" a girl's voice sang out from somewhere inside.

Freddie groaned. "Toasted cheese sandwich." He slammed down the lid. "It just isn't our day for kitchens, Tim!"

"You can say *that* again!" Tim told Freddie about the money, the two weeks' ban on video games, and the library bit.

Freddie looked sympathetic.

"Oh, no! Join the library? She can't do this to you!"

"You try telling *her* that!" said Tim. "Anyway, I'm on my way there now."

He didn't mention anything about his hopes concerning the new librarian or even about J. G.'s suspicions. The possibility of Freddie's being a suspect might be a very delicate subject right now.

Freddie looked troubled already.

"I'll come with you. I might as well check out the video department." He brightened a little. "Hey, maybe that's what you could do. Instead of messing with books."

Tim shook his head. "No chance . . . . She says I have to get the librarian to sign a note to say I've joined."

"Yeah, well . . ." Freddie turned. "Hey, kids, I'm just going along with Tim to the library—"

"Ooh, hurray! The library!"

There was a rush to the door.

"We'll come, too!"

Tim hadn't expected such excitement. And as the kids skipped and scampered around the boys like three frisky puppies, he couldn't help grinning.

Then his grin faded. He'd just spotted a figure standing close to a tree at the edge of the main street. It was J. G. The boy was staring up at the branches as if he'd seen a rare bird. He didn't turn his head as the three noisy girls drew closer. He couldn't have been more riveted if the bird had been a pterodactyl.

But Tim wasn't fooled.

At this distance he couldn't see the exact direction of J. G.'s gaze. But he felt sure of one thing. Even though J. G.'s head was stretched back and his hand was shading his eyes, those eyes would be flitting constantly to the approaching group. Especially the keen gray eye.

He—and Freddie—were being watched.

"What's *he* doing?" murmured Freddie as they passed closer.

"Who knows?" said Tim, still not wanting to alarm his friend. "He seems to have seen something up in the tree. Maybe a squirrel."

"If you ask *me,* he seems to be watching us," said Freddie, whose eyes were sharper than most kids'. "Is he with *you?*"

Tim shrugged. "*That* screwball! Forget him."

So they kept going.

Freddie's sisters were all younger. Ruth was ten, Julie nine, and Robyn eight. They were all very thin, with hungry-looking faces like Freddie's. Ruth and Julie had the same dark brown hair.

Robyn's was fair. They wore it in braids, which flew about as they danced and skipped.

Ruth wasn't quite as active as the others. "Always with her nose in a book," Freddie used to say. "It's why she wears glasses."

He spoke as if reading wasn't healthy. But like Tim, Ruth was a couple of inches taller than Freddie. In fact, Freddie wasn't much taller than Robyn. There was a rumor that he'd begun life growing normally, but then he'd slowed down when Mr. Fisher was sent to prison.

Usually the girls were fairly subdued, too. But not now.

"*They're* enthusiastic!" said Tim.

"Yeah," grunted Freddie. "It's the new librarian. Got 'em *all* hooked on books now."

"Oh, yes? This—uh—Felicity Snell?"

"Yeah. They're always talking about her. Felicity this, Felicity that!"

Julie and Ruth pricked up their ears.

"Felicity Snell's terrific!" said Ruth.

"You bet!" said Julie. "Felicity can do *anything*!"

"She tells us stories!" said Robyn.

"And draws pictures of the characters," said Ruth. "In front of us. In a *flash*!"

"And makes them look like *us kids*," added Robyn.

"The *good* ones, she does," said Julie. "The bad people she makes look like some of the grown-ups."

"Yeah. Like Mr. Snerdoff, the janitor," said Ruth.

"And that makes us laugh," said Julie.

"And *scream*!" said Robyn joyfully. "When it's scary."

"And once she made me *cry*," said Ruth proudly. "When it was a sad story."

"And she showed me a book about tap dancing," said Robyn.

"Then she did the steps herself to help me. Out in the lobby where there's no carpet."

"Felicity used to be a real dancer," said Julie. "On the stage."

"In New York," said Ruth. "Ballet, too," she added, beginning to walk on the tips of her toes and twirl around on the strip of grass next to the sidewalk.

"Look where you're going!" grunted Freddie. He'd not been doing much of that himself. He'd been glancing over his shoulder. "You sure that jerk isn't following us?"

Tim turned. J. G. wasn't far behind them, still staring up at the trees.

"Nargh!" said Tim, trying to sound calmer than he felt. "Looks like he's on some kind of vacation assignment. Doing a squirrel count, perhaps."

"Felicity knows about acrobatics, too," said Julie.

They'd now reached the part of West Milbury called The Green. Here the grass strips widened out between the busy modern road and the big old-fashioned houses.

The girls really began to show off here. Cartwheels, forward rolls, backward rolls, handstands, tumbles of all kinds on the still-wet grass.

"Hey, cut it out!" yelled Freddie. "You'll get soaked!"

But they took no notice. Only when one of the largest of the old houses loomed in sight at the curve of the road did they pick themselves up and go running on ahead, laughing and squealing. This was the Ebenezer Twitchpurse Memorial Library.

Tim Kowalski slowed down. . . .

He'd been past the library before, of course. He'd been inside the building, too. But that was mainly on school visits, when they'd been to see exhibitions in the museum or the art gallery. He'd even gone inside the Junior Lending Department on one of these visits, but that was long before the new librarian had arrived.

He remembered Freddie's whispered comment.

"Like a morgue. But with books instead of bodies."

The three little kids were scampering up the wide front steps. But just when they started to push through the main door they suddenly stopped, in a shrinking bunch, their happy cries fading in their throats.

"Looks like they've seen a ghost," said Tim.

"Yeah," murmured Freddie. "Or *worse*! Whenever I play Doctor Tongue's Castle of Terror down at the arcade, I think of this place."

"I see what you mean," said Tim, beginning to sound as glum as his friend. "They're going on inside, anyway."

The last of the sisters was just disappearing, steered by the protective arm of Ruth, who was clutching her book as if to shield Robyn's head from the talons and beak of some great guardian bird of prey.

"Yeah . . . ," gloomed Freddie.

It was still an uncertain kind of day, with black clouds piling up behind the library. There were lights on inside, but they only seemed to make the old Victorian ivy-covered front of the building gloomier.

Looming up behind was the more modern flat-roofed extension that housed the museum and art gallery. This part seemed even *more* sinister, despite its brighter lights. Its pale gray concrete walls looking very ghostlike against the black clouds.

Tim sighed.

"Yeah, well . . ." He took out his mother's note. "Let's get this over with, huh?"

6

The Guardian Ogre—and the Guardian Angel

"Hold it right there, pilgrims!"

Tim had never been called a pilgrim before. He knew what it meant. A kind of traveler going on a dangerous journey. Once, at Sunday school, they'd had a board game called The Pilgrim's Progress. It was about this pilgrim making his way to heaven. If he landed on a bad square, he found his way barred by giants, or ogres, or devils. If he landed on a good square, he was helped by angels, or maybe an old monk.

The square he and Freddie had now arrived on was the big rubber mat just inside the lobby. Then this barked command. They were both shocked. Freddie more than Tim, perhaps. Pilgrim's Progress hadn't been turned into a video game and *he* probably didn't know what a pilgrim was.

There was no doubt about who was addressing them, though, as they stared up. And up. And up . . .

This was a giant, all right! A giant who was also an ogre. A kid-eater.

Tim judged him to be at least six-foot-six. His face was as brown and leathery as an old boot: not much forehead and huge jutting jaws. His crew-cut hair was white, stiff, and bristly. The hair on his chest was white, too. It curled and bristled over the top of his sweat shirt. It reminded Tim of the steel wool stuff his mother scrubbed pans with.

Pinned to his shirt was the name tag:

	ERNEST SNERDOFF JANITOR
E T **LIBRARY**	

His arms were covered with tattoos. Crossed swords, the letters USMC, the word MOM.

The huge right hand was bunched up in a fist with the thumb hitched in the belt. The left held a squeegee mop, the mop end of which rested on the floor at the side of his massive combat boot. Like the rifle of an armed guard.

Freddie's fingers and thumbs were working overtime as he gaped up. Tim guessed his friend was busy with an imaginary video-game joystick, desperately trying to combat this monster with Thrust Kicks and Spinning Knuckles—in vain. *Nothing* looked as if it would make any impression on that guy.

He spoke again in that grating, menacing voice.

"Make sure you wipe them feet, pilgrims! I only just cleaned this floor!"

"Yes, *sir*!" Tim wiped his feet many times, fast. So did Freddie.

No wonder the Fisher girls had been pulled up short! To them, Ernest Snerdoff must have seemed all of ten feet tall.

And as the boys wiped away on the mat, like a couple of small white rats on an exercise wheel, Tim looked around.

To the left, a doorway marked: Adult Lending Department. Straight ahead: Video Department. And to the right, across a stretch of newly cleaned black and white tiles, the goal *these* two pilgrims had been making for: the Junior Lending Department. With glimpses of bright lights, pictures, books, shelves, tables, kids, and a woman with golden hair, a warm radiant smile, and a red shirt.

Tim suddenly felt as if they must have thrown a pair of sixes in the Pilgrim game.

"Okay," said the giant, in a grudging voice, "you can go in *now*."

"Me," said Freddie, making straight for the video department, "I'm going in *here*."

Tim paused at the entrance to the junior room.

There was a woman behind the counter. But Tim kept his attention focused on the one with the golden hair and red shirt. She was surrounded by a huddle of little kids, over in a corner. She was crouched in front of Robyn. Robyn was sobbing, her face wet with tears. Neither she nor her sisters took any notice of Tim.

"Right. Leave this to me, honey," said the woman. She gave Robyn a hug and came over to the door. She was wearing a pair of faded light blue jeans. She, too, had a name tag.

But as she came closer, Tim's attention was drawn higher—to the most vivid, most penetrating violet-blue eyes he'd ever seen.

They met his and she smiled.

"Excuse me." She marched past him, out into the lobby, followed by the still sniffling Robyn, her sisters, and some of the other kids. Then she said "Excuse me!" again. This time her voice was less gentle. "Mr. Snerdoff! Do you have a minute?"

Now that he knew for sure who she was, Tim examined those jeans with keener interest. Something told him they were old favorites—maybe a lucky pair that she couldn't bring herself to throw away: washed and washed and, yes, even patched here and there.

He wondered how many of those undercover detective missions she'd worn them on.

Tim saw her reach up under the red shirt to one of the back pockets. It was only to tuck away a bunch of damp tissues she'd been drying Robyn's eyes with. But Tim couldn't help wondering if that was the pocket where she kept the gun with which she'd had to shoot a man.

Ernest Snerdoff seemed uneasy about meeting those violet-blue eyes.

"This," she said, placing a hand on Robyn's head, "is a little girl, Mr. Snerdoff. Age eight. Weighing less than seventy pounds and measuring less than three-and-a half feet in height. She is *not* a six-foot recruit at boot camp, age eighteen and weighing *one hundred and seventy pounds*. . . . Yet you have terrified her. Why?"

The janitor's eyes flickered.

"They—she—they was walking on my clean floor."

"*Your* clean floor, Mr. Snerdoff?"

He nodded. "Without wiping their feet," he muttered.

"He didn't give us the *chance!*" Ruth piped up.

"*Your* clean floor, Mr. Snerdoff?" Felicity repeated.

"Well, the floor I'd just cleaned."

"And you stop *all* the visitors like that?"

A man and a woman had just entered and were heading for the adult department. Just behind them, almost as if he were *with* them, J. G. Farrell came in, too. If he was still playing detective, the kid certainly knew how to blend in, thought Tim, admiring the smooth way J. G. veered away from the man and woman and sloped off into the junior room. Unchallenged by Snerdoff, virtually unseen by anyone.

"Well, adults *know* to wipe their feet," said the janitor. "Kids is always leaving their tracks if you don't watch them and—"

"So *you* bawl them out? Scare the living daylights out of them? Shame on you, Mr. Snerdoff!" Felicity was looking at his left arm. "I always thought the U.S. Marines was for the *protection* of little kids." The janitor hung his head.

"Sorry, Ms. Snell. I guess you're right," he mumbled.

"You *know* I am, Mr. Snerdoff. But I can understand your getting carried away. Nobody else could *ever* get the floor this clean. I'm always saying to the chief librarian, 'You could eat your lunch off the floor when Mr. Snerdoff's through cleaning it!' "

"Gee, thanks, Ms. Snell!" said the janitor, his face lighting up. "It's because I use Old Squelcher here." He gave the mop handle an affectionate pat. "He gets in all the cracks and corners. Beats all yer state-of-the-art electric floor-polishing gizmos."

He turned to Robyn.

"Sorry, kid," he mumbled. "Me and Squelcher didn't mean to scare ya!"

"That's okay," said Robyn, staring wide-eyed at the mop.

Back in the junior room, Felicity turned to Tim.

"Hi! Welcome to the junior library. I'm Felicity Snell, the new librarian. *You're* new here, too, aren't you?"

Tim nodded. All this talk of muddy footprints had reminded him of what he'd really come for. He'd admired the way she'd handled the trouble in the lobby. But this still didn't prove she was the Wonder Sleuth his mom had made her out to be.

He took a deep breath and answered her question with another.

"If *you're* new here, ma'am, how d'you know *I'm* new?"

7

Felicity's X-Ray Eyes?

"That's a good question!" said Felicity.

Seeing her from the side while she'd been talking to the janitor, Tim had thought there was something sharp and beaklike about her nose. But right now he was beginning to wonder if he'd only imagined it.

"And the answer's this," she was saying. "I could tell by the way you looked at Elaine there, as if you weren't quite sure *she* wasn't the librarian."

"Well—" Tim glanced toward the counter and wasn't surprised to see J. G. Farrell there already, talking to the young woman and making her laugh about something. One real cool dude, thought Tim.

"She's my aide, as it happens. But you'd been told to see the children's librarian herself, hadn't you? Your parents *ordered* you to come here and join, right?"

Tim blinked, completely forgetting J. G. for the moment. Now this *was* a detective! "How—how did you know *that*?"

"Because of the note you were holding."

"Oh—uh—yeah. . . ." Tim plucked it out of his pocket. "But you couldn't read what it said from right over there, could you?"

She laughed. "No. But I could see the dotted line at the bottom. That's for me to sign on, isn't it?"

Tim nodded, stunned.

"Thank you." Felicity took it from him. "Yes. . . ."

She read it aloud, in a low voice.

" 'Please sign below to say Timothy Kowalski came to the library, then joined and stayed at least two hours, obliging his Mom, Jane Kowalski (Mrs.). Many thanks. P.S. Hope the perm that you had at Cuts 'n' Curls last week was okay.
    YES. TIMOTHY CAME & JOINED.
        Signed...
        Time............................ Date....................' "

Felicity looked at him, and Tim became aware of the penetrating quality of those eyes. *Ultra*-violet, as he was coming to think of them. X-ray eyes, from which no secrets could be hidden!

Felicity continued: "Ah, yes! I see the resemblance now. Your face has the same bone structure as hers. I was wrong about parents plural, though. You have only one. Your father died in an accident at work three years ago, right?"

Tim nodded sadly. She was scanning his forehead.

"You had chicken pox last year and you nearly drove your mother nuts picking at the spots. I can see the scars on your forehead. Yes, and the big one on your chin."

Tim fingered them, wondering how she knew about *them*.

"She even threatened to make you wear boxing gloves if you didn't stop. But she doesn't hold it against you. She says no kid could have looked after his mom better when she was in bed with the flu last March."

"How—how did you—?"

"Know all that? Your mom talks a lot, that's how. Especially when she has a really tricky head of hair like mine to work on." Felicity glanced down at the note. "Tell her the perm's holding up fine, by the way. . . . Hey!" Her eyes had switched from the note to his hands. "And I can see what she meant about you being hooked on video games."

"She told you *that*?"

"Yes. But I can tell just by the way you've been looking at my face. Left to right, back to left, up, down, over to right, up again, across, down . . . as if it was a video screen. And look at your fingers and thumb, right hand. Pressing imaginary buttons all the time. You don't even know you're doing it, do you?"

Tim was amazed. He thrust his hands out of sight. He *didn't* even know he'd been doing it. But he could believe it, so soon after seeing Freddie gaping up at Ernest Snerdoff.

"Gosh! You *must* have been a good detective, Ms. Snell! You don't miss a clue!"

"Call me Felicity. . . . Your mom told you about that, did she? Well, I guess libraries and detective work go together."

"Oh?"

"Yes. Books are all about clues. I mean what's reading but looking at marks on paper, like a hunter looking for prints in the snow?"

"Yes, but I was meaning *real* clues. Like in a real mystery. Like in the sneak-theft we just had at our house."

"Sneak-theft?" Suddenly Felicity's face set hard and hawklike.

"Yeah!" said Tim. "A—an *intruder*-theft."

Felicity's eyes narrowed.

"Tell me more . . . ," she murmured, leading the way to a vacant table and pointing to a chair.

Just then, J. G. broke off his conversation, saying, "Okay, Elaine. I'll tell Mary you were asking after her. But right now there's something I have to look up. See ya!"

8

Felicity Asks Questions

Felicity listened in silence as Tim began his account.

She glanced across at the three Fisher girls when he mentioned Freddie. She smiled when he described Hippo.

But her eyes became serious again when he came to the missing money.

"Did you know about the stash?"

"No. It was the first time I'd heard of it."

"Did your friend know?"

"How could he, if even I didn't?"

"Okay, Tim. Take it easy. . . . *Somebody* knew about it. If the popper was the only thing stolen and the thief went straight for it. But you said there were clues?"

When Tim told her about the footprints, Felicity's nose seemed to sharpen. And when he described the small heaps of sugarlike substance, her eyes narrowed.

"Like brown sugar?"

"Yes. That crunchy kind. Not the powdery stuff we usually have."

"So if it *was* sugar, it had been brought in by the thief?"

"Yes."

"Interesting!" Then suddenly Felicity opened her eyes wide. "Did your mom sweep them up?"

"Uh-uh! She said to leave them for the police."

Felicity seemed relieved.

"Did they say when they'd be coming?"

Tim told her how the cop had promised there'd be someone stopping by before the weekend.

"He said they'd be sending Detective Delaney."

Felicity frowned. "And you say the boy with you was Freddie Fisher?"

"Yes." Tim sighed. "I don't know whether you know, ma'am—"

"*Felicity*, please! . . . About his father?" she added, with a quick anxious glance at Freddie's sisters. "Yes. I do know."

"Well, it was Detective Delaney, four years ago, who—"

"Yes," she cut in, with a sad, troubled look. "I know about that, too."

Up to this point, kids had kept sidling up to ask her things or tell her things. Tim guessed at first they'd been trying to get in on the act. Kids who were jealous she was giving him so much of her time.

But others were plain curious. They'd come to snoop. A few had genuine queries. One—a rather dumb kid in Tim's class at school, named Spencer—had been helping to put books back on the shelves. He wasn't sure where some of them should go. A girl had come with an open book and a fink look, eager to show Felicity where someone's baby brother or sister had scribbled with a red pencil.

Felicity had handled these threatened interruptions like a cop directing traffic, without breaking off her conversation with Tim. She seemed to know what the genuine queries were about before the kids had time to explain. She only had to glance at Spencer's books before pointing to the right shelves. Holly Jenks, the girl with the scribbled-on book, was redirected to Elaine with a word of thanks. The others were staved off with an upraised hand and a murmured "Later!" All done with a friendly smile. That seemed to be all they'd come for, anyway.

One thing puzzled Tim. The fact that J. G. didn't seem to be one of the snoopers. At first he wasn't anywhere to be seen.

Tim was beginning to think that J. G. must have been telling the truth when he'd told Elaine he had something to look up. Perhaps he was doing just that, out of sight behind one of the stacks. Maybe he really had seen some strange bird up in the trees. Maybe he was trying to identify it.

The only interruption that took Felicity by surprise was when a squeal went up in the far corner.

"Hey! It's Freddie! Where you been, Freddie? Over here, Freddie!"

It was Robyn, with Ruth trying to hush her.

Freddie was at the entrance, crimson-faced.

Felicity smiled.

"If it isn't Game Boy himself!" she said as he came across. "Don't tell me *you've* come to join the library, Freddie?"

"Not right now, ma'am." He turned to Tim. "I was just thinking. How will your mom know you didn't get some other kid to come in your place? Someone else who hasn't been here before?"

Felicity was looking at him curiously. Tim hoped she wasn't thinking his friend had a criminal mind, coming out with such a cunning suggestion!

"Felicity saw at once I really was Tim Kowalski," he said hurriedly. "Same bone structure in my face as Mom's."

"Just as I can see *you're* a Fisher," said Felicity. "Same bones as your sisters. Especially Ruth's."

Freddie was now gaping at her.

"She even knew about—" Tim stopped. He'd been about to say "—your father." He quickly changed it to "—my chicken pox."

"Anyway—" Felicity signed the note and fixed her violet-blue gaze on Freddie. "What I'm *really* interested in right now is what Tim's been telling me about the corn popper. You were there too, I understand?"

Freddie swallowed hard. "Y-yes, ma'am."

"Okay." Felicity brought in Tim with a glance that was just as piercing. "So now we'll go over it again. With exact times." She got up. "Excuse me while I get a notepad."

She went over to the counter. Then, as she picked up a large yellow pad, Tim nudged his friend and murmured:

"Looks like we're in business, Freddie!"

"Uh—yeah. . . ." Freddie didn't sound too happy.

9

The Three Kinds of Clues

"I *hate* sneak-thieves!" said Felicity as she sat down. "They put every innocent person who happens to be around under suspicion."

"Yeah!" said Tim. "Like with the corn popper!"

"Exactly!" Felicity clicked her pen. She headed the page *Stolen Article* and jotted down the details that Tim had already given her, like Hippo's shape and size.

"You say he's bright green with a red cap?"

"Yes."

Felicity added those details, saying, "Should be easy enough to spot, anyway!" Then she looked up. "Now let's see if we can narrow down the time. When did your mom leave?"

"Eight twenty-five. As usual."

"Okay. So what did you do then?"

"I went upstairs to get the game set up."

Felicity nodded and went on writing.

"Then what?"

"Then Freddie arrived."

"Yeah, at exactly eight forty-five," said his friend. "And Tim *had* locked the door that time. I had to hammer on it to get him to hear."

"I was trying out the game with the sound track turned up."

Felicity raised her eyebrows.

"But you heard Freddie all the same?"

"Only when I hammered real loud," Freddie insisted.

"Anyway," said Felicity, turning to Tim, "you then went down and let him in?"

"Sure."

"And did you lock the door after *that*?"

"I—uh—guess not. . . ."

Felicity wrote: *Door left unlocked from 8:45 onward.* Then came a longer note:

8:45 — ? Boys up in Tim's room taking turns to try out Driver and Shooter roles, and generally getting familiar with the game.

"You'd be very absorbed by this time, I suppose," said Felicity. "*Did* you hear anything down below?"

They shook their heads.

Felicity hesitated before asking the next question.

"Did either of you leave the room for anything?"

"Yes," Freddie answered promptly. "Bathroom."

"Upstairs or down?'

"Upstairs."

"But *I* went down," said Tim. "At the same time. To get a couple of Cokes."

"And that was around—when?"

Tim perked up. "Oh, at ten forty-five. I noticed the time on the microwave clock. I remember being surprised it was that late."

Felicity nodded. "Good. And on the other side of the microwave—isn't that where you said Hippo had his place?"

"Yes."

45

"And was it still there?"

"Sure. I'd have been certain to notice if it had gone already."

"Good!" said Felicity again. "So that narrows it down nicely. The popper wasn't stolen until after ten fifty. . . . Did either of you go down after that?"

"No," said Tim.

"So you didn't surface until your mother arrived home at twelve oh-five and discovered the theft?"

Sadly, Tim shook his head.

Felicity ended this section with:

Thief strikes between 10:50 and 12:05.

"Just over an hour," she murmured. "Now for the other details." She turned to Freddie. "Tim tells me neither of you knew about the money."

"No, ma'am. *I* didn't, anyway."

Then Felicity Snell asked a very strange question.

"Where do you get your hair cut, Freddie?"

Freddie blinked. So did Tim.

"Sam's Barbershop," said Freddie. "Why?"

"You never go to Cuts 'n' Curls then?"

"Nargh! Mainly women and girls go there! Too expensive, anyway. Why?"

"Oh, nothing," murmured Felicity.

The boys looked at each other. Maybe she's losing her grip on the case, thought Tim.

Felicity gave her head a brisk wake-up shake. Then she began to ask about the footprints and the heaps of brown crystals. She seemed especially interested in pinning down the exact positions of these things, print by print and (almost) grain by grain.

By now Tim was beginning to notice a difference in the movements of the other kids. Most of them still looked enviously at all the attention Tim and now Freddie were getting from Felicity. No one came up and asked Felicity questions. But they were all obviously curious, dying to find out what all the fuss was about with the questions and notes.

Spencer seemed to have found another bunch of books to replace on the shelves. But he wasn't bringing them from the counter. He must have found them on a book wagon somewhere around the back of the stack behind Felicity. That was where he kept coming from, anyway. And someone seemed to be giving him a hand. Twice he was pulled back by another person, out of sight behind the stack, and more books were thrust into his hands.

Tim wondered at first if it was Elaine. But no. She was still busy at the counter, dealing with kids as they came in to return books or take new ones out. Holly Jenks was up there, too, lending Elaine a hand with some vases of wildflowers. She came up to the table they were sitting at with a bunch of chicory, but Felicity waved her away with a gentle murmur of, "Not now, Holly. And be careful not to spill any water."

She was still preoccupied with the details about the footprints and the spilled sugar.

"And I do mean *exact*," she said, when it became clear neither boy could be precise enough. "So what I need now is for you both to go back and take a closer look. Draw a plan of the kitchen counter and the floor and mark the positions of these things, plus measurements." She looked at Tim. "Do you have a magnifying glass, by any chance?"

Tim's heart beat faster at the mention of this basic tool of the detective's trade. "I'm not sure."

Then his eyes narrowed. Holly had just placed the vase of chicory on top of the book stack. Then, as if she, too, had been working with an invisible helper, a hand reached up from the other side and quietly readjusted the vase, pushing it closer to the space just to the right of the back of Felicity's head.

Tim checked quickly, but no. It wasn't Elaine who was making the rearrangement. *She* was still at the counter. And when he turned back, it was to see the flowers themselves being readjusted, with the fingers of the mysterious hand busy among them, making a gap in the middle through which could now be seen a pair of eyes: one gray, one brown. J. G. Farrell's.

Oh, sure, The Kids' Own Detective was busy with his "looking up." Or rather looking *down*—straight at Felicity's notepad!

"Never mind," said Felicity, still talking about the magnifying glass. "I have one here I can lend you."

"Magnifying glass?" Freddie's eyes were wide.

"Yes. I want you to check those prints for even the faintest trace of a pattern. . . ." Felicity thought for a moment. "But if there isn't one, don't worry. That could be the most important clue of all. It could tell us—"

"Oops!" gasped a voice from the other side of the stack.

This caused Felicity to look up curiously, just in time to see a hand grab the vase and steady it.

"Mind what you're doing back there! We don't want another waterfall down the shelves. Why don't you empty some more water out, Holly, before there's an accident?"

"Yes, ma'am," said the crimson-faced girl who'd come back just in time to see the near disaster. Her eyes were still popping.

But Tim was too engrossed with Felicity's last remarks about the footprints and their lack of pattern to pay much attention to snoopers like J. G. Farrell.

"Why could blank footprints be so important?" he asked.

"Just check," was all Felicity replied. "Make accurate sketches. And as soon as possible. Before they get disturbed or wiped away.

Your mother might forget and—"

"Oh, she won't do that before Detective Delaney's been! She said so herself."

"She might be busy with cooking or —" Felicity broke off. "What's wrong, Freddie?"

Freddie was staring at Tim, looking scared, alarmed. "*Him? Delaney?* You didn't tell *me* that!"

Felicity now seemed to realize what was eating him.

"Don't worry, Freddie. Rick Delaney isn't the type to start blaming every person in sight. Anyway, by the time he gets around to visiting we could have solved the case ourselves. I'm already building up a picture of what *kind* of person did it."

"You *are?*" said Freddie.

"Yes, but I do need more details." Felicity tore out the notes. "Here's the list of what I want you to check."

Freddie grabbed the sheets and started poring over them.

"Are these marks to show where you want us to use the magnifying glass, ma'am?" He was pointing to some small doodle-type drawings in the margin.

Felicity laughed. "No. That's just my own private code. Clues that could be especially important. A magnifying glass with the letter *c* in it."

"But they aren't all alike," said Tim.

"No," said Felicity. "There are three different kinds. Like this. . . ."

They watched as she drew them again on the next page, this time much larger.

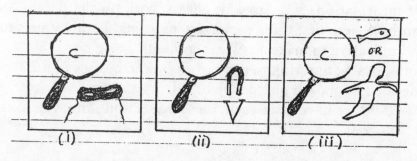

"Number one, with the small black mask, indicates a clue that a criminal leaves by accident. A clue that might lead to identifying him. Or her."

"Hey, yeah!" said Freddie. "You've put one here, next to the footprints."

"So what's this second one for?" said Tim. "With the horseshoe and the V?"

"That's a *magnet*, Tim. That's what I call a *victim* clue. A clue left by the victim that attracts the criminal. Like letting him know there's something worth stealing. Or that it'll be easy."

"But you've put one next to the note about us being up in Tim's room after eight forty-five," Freddie murmured.

"Correct! Making a lot of noise. Letting the thief know that stealing something from the kitchen would be easy. A victim clue."

Tim quickly pointed to the third sketch.

"What—?"

"The one with the fish or the spook is what I call a *phantom* clue. A clue left to put people off the scent. A.k.a. a red herring."

"To mislead the cops, right?" said Freddie, grinning.

"Not always. Sometimes it's used to mislead neighbors or other possible witnesses."

The boys looked puzzled.

"And you've put one here, next to the sugar spills note," Tim said. "If it *is* sugar."

"Yes," said Felicity. "But with a query. I'm not sure until I get more information. . . . Anyway, get to work on the details and report back here first thing tomorrow morning. Before it gets too busy. I may have to make a few experiments. . . ."

Both boys were raring to start work but before they left, Freddie decided to make a photocopy of Felicity's notes.

"We'd better have a set each," he said, leading the way to the machine in the lobby. But he wasn't followed only by Tim.

Ruth, Julie, and Robyn weren't far behind. For the last few minutes they'd been watching, wide-eyed, while Felicity had been making her notes and explaining her signs. They'd also been listening intently, but Felicity had kept her voice low and they were burning with curiosity.

"What is it, Freddie?" asked Ruth as they crossed the lobby. "Has Felicity been telling you a story? What about?"

"Yeah!" Julie chimed in. "Tell us, Freddie! What are the pictures she's drawn?"

"Is it a ghost story?" said Robyn, making a grab at the sheet with the phantom clue sketch.

Freddie paid no attention to them, except to lift the notes high out of Robyn's reach. He had the knack of being able to shut out the kids completely, as if they were no more than a bunch of gnats.

Fired by what Felicity had said, eager to get down to business, he concentrated on making good clear copies, and as he and Tim left to go on their way he didn't even seem to notice the three girls squabbling over the handful of rejects he'd tossed into the trash bin.

And he *certainly* didn't notice J. G. Farrell loping over toward the machine, with head bent forward like a cat stalking mice. He didn't notice Ernest Snerdoff, either, scowling at the kids from the entrance to the adult department. Waste papers were already littering the floor next to the bin.

"Hey!" growled the janitor. "Keep outa there, youse kids! Keep the place neat!"

"That's okay, Mr. Snerdoff," said J. G., already stooping down. "I'll clear it up. I guess their brother has too much on his mind to keep the brats in order," he added darkly, smoothing out one of the crumpled rejects and frowning down at it, his gray right eye glittering like quicksilver.

10

The New Clue

"Hey! Someone's lost a tooth!"

The two boys had just come back from the library. Each had his copy of Felicity's notes. Freddie was clutching the magnifying glass she'd lent them. Both were still eager to get on with the investigation. But they hadn't even reached the door of the Kowalski house. They hadn't even entered the backyard.

Freddie had stopped at the end of the path. He was bending over a small white object on the ground at the side. Tim marveled at Freddie's sharp eyes. He himself might easily have missed it.

"Looks like a molar," he said.

"Yeah," grunted Freddie. "Worth a coupla dimes of any tooth fairy's money. It isn't one of yours, is it?"

Tim shook his head. "Looks bigger than mine, anyway. More like an adult's."

He bent closer, then suddenly laughed.

"Molar, nothing!" he said, picking it up. "This is a piece of popcorn." Then his grin faded. "Hey! Popcorn of the nonsticky kind! The healthy kind!"

"Wow!" said Freddie. "I bet I know where *that's* come from. This could be important evidence." He held out his hand. "Let me see!" He brought the glass up close to it. "How long is it since you made any popcorn in Hippo?"

"Months." Tim thought about it. "It could be a piece left over from that time. Not fully popped. A piece not spewed out with the rest."

"Yeah," said Freddie. "Look. What I thought was part of the molar's roots. It's really the unpopped part of the kernel. See the sharp end. I'm gonna draw this when we get inside. We'll show it to Felicity. See what *she* makes of it."

Here is a copy of his drawings, with the measurements Tim added.

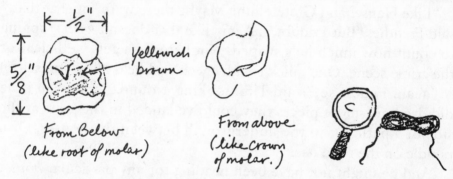

From Below
(like root of molar)

From above
(like Crown
of molar.)

"I think I know already what Felicity will say," murmured Tim. "That it must have been left inside Hippo's heat chamber and gotten mixed up with the bills in Mom's stash."

"Right!" said his friend. "And you know what that means, don't you?"

"What?"

"That the thief couldn't wait to check the money. He must have had Hippo concealed in a bag of some kind. But when he got this far he just *had* to reach in, remove Hippo's head, and grope about for the stash."

He made the movements as he spoke, using an imaginary bag and looking around guiltily, as if afraid of being observed. Just the way a real thief *would* act.

"So?" Tim said.

"So when he pulled the stash out, the corn dropped out without him even noticing."

Tim nodded. After that point the road took several directions away from the yard. The thief could have been heading in any one of them, with other paths leading to other houses, including the Farrell house opposite.

"If only there'd been some more stray pieces," he said. "They might have made a trail leading to the thief."

"Like Hansel and Gretel, huh? Maybe there were some at that," said Freddie. "But I doubt it. A guy like that doesn't *keep* stopping to count how much he's swiped. Not before he gets well clear of the crime scene. One quick rough check's all he'd allow himself."

"Yeah. I guess so," said Tim, looking around. "And even if he did drop any more pieces they could've landed in the grass at the side of a path. Or in the undergrowth between the houses. Or a puddle on the road itself."

"And he might not have been heading for any particular *house*. Maybe—" Freddie stopped. "*Hey . . .* " he drawled slowly. "It does tell us one thing definite!" He was gently rolling the popcorn around in the palm of his hand. "It's dry. It couldn't have been dropped until after the heavy shower. Felicity'll be interested in *that*. Helps to confirm the time of the theft."

Cheered up some by this, the boys were just moving off toward the back door when they were arrested by a shrill yell.

"Hey! Wait! Wait till you hear *this*!"

It was Ruth, eyes wide, running up from the main street. She looked and sounded indignant as well as excited. Close on her heels came the other two girls, just as excited, but bewildered rather than mad.

"Not now, Ruth," said Freddie, making gnat-brushing movements. "We're busy investigating a crime."

"That's just it," said Ruth, blinking hard behind her glasses. "You're not the only ones! Wait till you hear who *else* is!"

11

J. G. Asks Questions

Tim stopped at the door. He had a nasty feeling that he knew the person Ruth was talking about.

"Who?" said Freddie.

"John Farrell, that's who!" said Ruth.

"Yeah, *him*!" chimed in Julie.

"And Holly Jenks," added Robyn.

"That *fink*!" said Ruth, nodding. "But mainly John Farrell."

"I knew it!" said Tim, looking anxiously at his friend.

At first Freddie wasn't all that concerned.

"Oh, him. That old J. G., he's always investigating something! Come on, Tim, open up. We have a *real* crime to investigate. A serious one."

"That's what John Farrell seems to think," said Ruth. "That's why he'd brung Holly Jenks as a witness."

"A witness to the *crime*?" asked Tim.

"No," said Ruth. "As a witness to him asking us questions."

"What questions?" asked Freddie. "What did he think you knew about it?"

"Plenty!" said Ruth, sounding grimmer than ever.

"When was this?" asked Tim.

"Just a few minutes ago," said Julie. "Outside the library."

"Near the fishpond," said Robyn.

"Yeah!" grunted Ruth. "I guess *he* was fishing."

They were referring to the pond in the library's garden of rest. It had a big stone statue of a dolphin leaping out of the water in the center. The kids called it "Jaws."

"Robyn always likes to see the goldfish when we go to the library," said Ruth.

"Pretty fish," said Robyn.

"That's all we were doing," said Julie. "When *he* came asking his questions."

"What questions?" repeated Freddie.

But Ruth took her time, making the most of her dramatic news. She set the scene first, describing how she and her sisters were sitting on the low stone parapet surrounding the pond.

"Then John Farrell and Holly Jenks came and sat on a bench nearby," said Ruth. "Kind of bossy and official. *She* just sat on the bench, anyway, ready to make her notes. But *he* sat on the backrest, all high and mighty, glaring down at us. He'd got a bunch of papers. Those you'd thrown in the bin under the photocopier."

"Those we thought at first was a story Felicity had been telling you," said Julie.

"A ghost story," said Robyn. "With the picture of a spook next to a ring. Only it wasn't a story."

"It was all the details you'd told her about the stolen corn popper," said Ruth.

Tim could picture the scene by the pond very clearly. He himself had once had questions fired at him by J. G. sitting ("all high and mighty" yes!) on the stoop in front of the Farrell house. About a stolen bicycle. Instead of papers, he'd been clutching an unlit pipe close to his chest. One of his father's, which he probably thought made him look like Sherlock Holmes. He'd been jumping the gun even then. Just because his sister's bike was missing, he'd built it up into a federal case involving a ring of international bike thieves.

Only to find out in the end that it had simply been borrowed by one of the girl's boyfriends to get home with late at night.

J. G. had been grounded then, too: (a) For causing an uproar over nothing, and (b) for borrowing his father's pipe without permission.

"The questions!" Freddie was saying now. "What was he asking? Come on!"

"His first question," said Ruth, "was, 'Have you heard about the robbery at the Kowalski house?' And I said, 'Yes, a corn popper.' Then, 'Anything else?' he said. And I said, 'Not that I know of.' That seemed to puzzle him and he said, 'Huh!' "

Julie took up the account then.

" 'How did *you* get to know about it?' was his next question."

"Yes," said Ruth. "So I said Freddie had told us when he came home to make lunch. And Robyn chipped in with, 'Which he burned and nearly set the kitchen on fire!' "

"And John Farrell said, 'Interesting! Note that, Holly!' But I think even *that* was going too fast for her." Ruth sniffed contemptuously. "It was the *next* question that really got to me!"

"Which was?" prompted Tim.

"He said, 'I guess Freddie was kind of nervous, was he? Burning the lunch like that? Maybe he was very preoccupied, was that it?' So then I said, 'Hey, what *is* this? Why are you asking *us*?' "

"She looked real mad!" said Julie. "I thought Ruth was going to up and shove him off that bench. Perched up like that, it would have been easy!" she added wistfully.

"Yeah! You *should* have, Ruth!" said Robyn.

Freddie still looked puzzled.

"Why? What was he getting at?"

Ruth ignored the question.

"He must have seen me looking mad. So he started backing off.

'Take it easy, Ruth,' he said. 'I'm only trying to be helpful. . . . Tim and Freddie have asked Felicity Snell to help find the thief. But what can *she* know at this distance? She didn't even know *Tim* before today. She doesn't know the Kowalski house where the crime took place. So we're just doing the job properly. Trying to fill in these details for her.' That's when he started reading through the notes he'd picked up from the trash can."

Freddie gasped. Tim groaned. Ruth went on with her account.

"So then I said, 'Did Felicity *ask* you to?' And all he could say was, 'Well, no. We're aiming to surprise her. Anyway, some detective she is! I live nearly opposite the Kowalski house and she hasn't asked me yet if I saw anyone suspicious hanging around.' "

Tim felt himself going tense.

Ruth continued. "So I said to John Farrell, 'Well—*did* you see anyone?' And he said, 'No. But I think maybe you did.' 'Me?' I said. And he said, 'Yes. You were in the vicinity. I saw you with a laundry bag. Bulky. Around eleven, after the rain had stopped. On the way to the Laundromat.' "

"And were you?" said Tim.

"Yeah." Ruth nodded. "Taking some things of Mom's to be cleaned. And like I said to him, 'So what if I was?' Then he said, 'Now note this carefully, Holly—' and he turned to me and said real slow: 'So did you see anyone acting suspiciously?' And I said, also real slow and clear, 'No, I did not see *anyone*—period!' But it didn't faze him. He said, 'Not anyone calling at the Kowalski house? Knocking on the door? Or maybe just stepping out of there?' And I said, 'No! How many more times? Anyway, how about *you*, Mr. Big Detective? Didn't *you* see anyone?'"

Tim sighed. "And what was his answer?"

"He said he wasn't looking especially. He didn't know about the crime then. So I shot it right back to him. 'Well, neither did I know about the crime then. So *I* wasn't looking especially, either.' Then he changed the subject."

Tim braced himself.

"How?"

"His next question," said Ruth, "was kind of strange. He said, 'Well, okay—so after he'd burned the lunch, did Freddie cheer up?' And I said, *'Huh?'* And he said, 'You know. Did he look pleased with himself?' 'What?' I said. 'About burning the *lunch*? Come *on!*' And he smiled that snooty smile, and said, 'No. Like maybe he had some good news. Like he'd just won a prize. Some money, maybe . . . I don't know. He'd share *that* with you, wouldn't he?' "

Ruth was now looking angry again.

"Instead of answering, I said it one more time: 'Hey! What *is* this?' I didn't like the way these questions were going."

"Me either!" growled Freddie. "So what did he say then?"

"He said maybe you were pleased because of some new video game you'd bought. Or maybe one you and Tim were planning to buy—a really superexpensive one. Maybe Tim had been given some extra birthday money and he'd just told Freddie the good news."

Tim gulped. Now *he*, too, was coming under J. G.'s cloud. Next jump of the gun and I'll be the joint prime suspect! he thought.

Freddie was now openly alarmed.

"The jerk! He thinks *I'm* the thief, doesn't he? And I think I know why!" he added grimly.

Ruth looked at him.

"Why? Not—not because of—?"

"Because of *Dad*? Yeah," said Freddie, his eyes blazing now. "He thinks I stole the money. Just because my father—" He choked up.

Tim put a hand on his friend's shoulder. "Take it easy, Freddie. The jerk thinks we *both* swiped the money, by the sound of it.

Anyway, forget *him*. Let's get down to work. Felicity's the *real* detective. And the sooner she has those details the sooner she'll find the real thief."

"Yeah!" said Ruth. "And the sooner—" Then she paused, her eyes going narrow. "*He-ey*!" she drawled. "I think he's watching us now! From his house!"

"Huh?" said Tim.

"At the bedroom window over the front door. He's watching us through binoculars. I saw the lenses flash in the sunlight."

Sure enough, when Tim came to look he saw the shadowy figure of J. G. Farrell hurriedly switch the direction of the glasses.

The girls' reaction was instantaneous. A combined show of contempt and defiance. Julie, the acrobat, turned her back on the Farrell house, did a smart handstand with a midair twist, and made quick kicking movements in the air. Robyn's best effort was to face the Farrell house, put her left thumb in her mouth and her right thumb in her right ear and wiggle all the free fingers furiously. Ruth, however, was cool and ladylike. She simply fixed the world's worst detective in her sights, took off her glasses, held them up with lenses pointing at the Farrell house, and thrust them slowly backward and forward.

"To show the creep we know he's been spying on us," she said.

12

The New Prime Suspect

Tim groaned inwardly. Freddie looked like joining the kids in their demonstration any minute. Tim could see the thing ending in a noisy full-scale siege of the Farrell house.

He steered Freddie to the kitchen door.

"Okay, kids!" he said. "Leave it to us now while we make the notes Felicity asked us for. Measurements of all the footprints and the heaps of sugary stuff."

That did it. They immediately turned.

"We can help you, we can help you, we'll come in, too!" the shrill chorus arose.

Tim thought of them trampling all over the footprints, dipping their wet fingers into the sugary piles, scattering the stuff all over the kitchen. He shuddered.

"Thanks, but we've got to do this carefully," he began. "We need to—"

"Yeah!" Freddie looked almost as alarmed as Tim. "You guys go and see if Mom's home yet. She might have brought us some candy. This is crime-scene forensic work. It needs a lot of careful measuring. Precision stuff. To the nearest hundredth, maybe *thousandth,* of an inch. You *know.*"

They didn't know, judging from the looks on their faces. But they sure were impressed by the words. Ruth nodded gravely and approached the door.

"Did it help? Us telling you about his questions?"

"Sure did!" said Tim. "It tells us we need to be on our guard. And to be quick and get this case solved."

"It tells us something else, too," Freddie said grimly. "It tells us we now have a likely prime suspect!"

Both Tim and Ruth turned.

"Who?" they asked.

"Why, *him* of course!" snapped Freddie. "That fink Farrell!"

"How—how d'you make *that* out?" asked Tim.

"Well . . . It's obvious." Freddie was breathing in angry jerks. "I mean it looks like . . . he's trying . . . to pin it on *me*, right?"

Tim shrugged. "Yes. On you and me both, in fact. But you think—?"

"That he's the real perpetrator? Sure. He's been casing your house. We've just seen him. With the binoculars. He could already have seen your mom stuffing her tips into Hippo. And he could have been watching *us* through them. Busy with the game this morning. He could have seen his chance and been over here in a flash. And now the money's disappeared he's doing his best to divert attention from himself to *us*!"

"But he doesn't even know the correct amount," said Tim. "He thinks it's over two thousand dollars and it's nowhere near!"

"Argh! That's just a blind! Just to make it look like he didn't know *too* much. An old crook's trick."

This time Tim groaned aloud. Here was *Freddie* jumping the gun like crazy!

"Come on, Freddie," he said gently. "The guy's a screwball, sure. But he's honest enough."

"Screwball—schmooball!" growled Freddie. "He could get me into very serious trouble with his lies!"

"Well, there's that," Tim had to admit.

"Yeah! Screwball—schmooball!" chimed in Julie and Robyn. This was the language they understood. Julie was already standing on her hands and twisting around to face the Farrell house again. Robyn's thumbs were moving back into her mouth and ear.

"And anyway I still think he's the perpetrator," said Freddie as the two younger girls began to make their cartwheeling, finger-wiggling way toward the Farrell house, still chattering, "Screwball, schmooball!"

"Well, it's one way of getting them out of *our* hair," Tim was thinking, when suddenly Ruth cried, "Uh-oh! Here comes Mr. Farrell! I'd better head them off!"

"Yeah, you do that, girl!" urged Freddie. "We don't want any more trouble with the grown-ups around here. Like that time you brung them trick-or-treating last year and someone called the cops!"

The boys stared at the scene in awe.

"This could be trouble!" murmured Tim.

The kids' cries had now hardened into a chant: *Screwball Farrell! Spitball, curveball, screwball Farrell!*

They were facing the house, yelling up at the window like small birds mobbing a marauding hawk. They didn't see the other people who started coming out of their houses to see what all the fuss was about. They didn't see Mrs. Rossi next door, with the baby, who was crying. They didn't see old Mr. Grant scowling across at them. They didn't even see Ms. Kilkinder from higher up the slope suddenly fling open her front door and glare down to see what was causing the ruckus.

And especially they didn't see Mr. Farrell, by now only a few feet behind them.

Mr. Farrell drove a truck. He delivered fuel oil for home heating. It was hard work at ordinary times. But in the summer months when people's tanks remained full except for a few gallons here and there, it was a tiring, irritating job. All that stopping and starting and connecting and disconnecting for next to nothing. It got him down. A guy still got sweaty and oily and thirsty, and when he finally called it a day, all he wanted was a long, cold shower and a long, cold, peaceful drink.

But what was *this*? A mob of kids yelling up at *his* house? The neighbors all rubbernecking?

He had a cheroot in his mouth. It had been there all afternoon. It wasn't lit. He'd stopped smoking weeks ago. But he liked to keep it there. It sort of steadied his nerves.

Best of all he enjoyed it when anyone said, "Hey, should you be smoking that? So close to the fuel lines and all?" Especially he enjoyed it if it should be a cop or a fire department volunteer.

Then he'd say, "Who says I'm *smoking* it? I've got my boots on but I ain't walking. You're kind of jumping the gun, aren't you, officer?"

This made him feel he was scoring one over that pesky gun-jumping son of his. He liked to tell the kid how many folks he'd had to correct over that little matter of the unlit cigar. There'd been two that day.

But now, as he chomped on the cigar and approached the steps up to his house, he forgot all about that.

"What goes on?" he bellowed.

He had to shout because by now Julie was in full swing. She was training herself to be a cheerleader and she could now turn anything into a chant.

"In curve.
Out curve.
Up curve.
Down curve.

Curve ball.
Spit ball.
*Screwball
Farrell!*"

she sang, prancing in front of the Farrell house, shaking her fists up at the window.

Robyn was already finding it tough to keep up. Mr. Farrell's bellow got through to her first.

"Eyeball, softball, gumball . . .," she faltered, and began to pluck Julie's sleeve.

Ruth stepped in.

"It's your John, Mr. Farrell. It's his fault. He started it."

"He's up there now," said Julie, quick to recover. "At the window."

"Doin' *what*?" roared Mr. Farrell.

"Accusing people," said Julie. "Accusing them of doing something they haven't done."

"Saying they was stealing!" said Robyn.

"Asking stupid questions!" said Julie.

"With Holly Jenks as witness writing the answers!" said Ruth.

"Saying we was stealing goldfish from the library pond!" said Robyn.

"Spying on other people's houses with binoculars!" said Ruth.

"Saying we was—we was—," faltered Robyn, not quite sure how to keep this going. Then: "Saying we was pushing people off the back of the bench so they fell. *And cracked their heads open!*" she added for full measure.

This was too much for Julie.

"He didn't accuse anyone of *that*, Robyn!"

"No, but he was *thinking* of it!" said Robyn.

Mr. Farrell stared from one to another bewildered. And no wonder. But the hard basic facts had already come through clearly enough.

Asking questions, huh? Writing down answers? Making wild accusations? Spying on neighbors with binoculars, *yet*? It all added up to the kind of dumb amateur detective work that had caused such grief in the past. *His son was at it again!*

"Okay. Clear off!" he said. "*I'll* deal with this. *Tfftt!*" (The cheroot was absolutely in tatters. That "Tfftt!" was Mr. Farrell spitting out the bits as he climbed the last three steps in one stride.)

"Looks like J. G.'s in for another grounding," said Tim.

"Serves the jerk right!" said Freddie. "I hope it's six weeks this time. And that'll be nothing compared to what he'll get when we prove he's the one who swiped Hippo!"

"*If* not *when*, Freddie," murmured Tim, steering him away from the door. "*If* we prove he's the one who swiped Hippo. Don't *you* start jumping the gun or we'll never get anywhere!"

13

Tim and Freddie Get Down to Work

Mrs. Kowalski came home that afternoon earlier than usual.

She paused when she saw the kitchen light was on. She cautiously tried the door. Unlocked. Maybe the sneak-thief's come back for a second helping, she thought. Right, buster!

She flung open the door, ready to rouse the neighborhood.

Then she stopped short.

It was only Tim. Back already. With Freddie Fisher, yet!

"I thought I told you no games!"

Tim was taking a couple of cans of Coke from the refrigerator. Always one of his first moves.

"Yes, Mom, but—"

"What's *he* doing here, then?"

Freddie was kneeling down. He had a magnifying glass, a sheet of paper, and a pencil.

"It isn't a game, Mom. It's a library assignment. Set by Felicity Snell. Here . . . " Tim handed her the signed note.

Freddie looked up. "Tim told her about Hippo and we're getting the exact details she asked for. Uh—be careful, Mrs. Kowalski. You're nearly treading on the evidence."

"Uh? . . . Oh—sorry!"

Mrs. Kowalski glanced down and sidestepped the spilled sugar-like stuff. Then she took the note from Tim.

The prints had dried a whitish color. They looked a lot clearer than when they were still wet.

"Felicity's taken our case, Mom!" Tim announced.

"We're measuring the clues for her," Freddie added.

Both boys had forgotten about J. G. by now. The careful, painstaking work had a wonderful calming effect. As Felicity told them later, this was always the way to go when faced with a baffling crime.

Mrs. Kowalski was beginning to look really pleased. "Wow! Do you know how much this would cost if she'd still been working for Coast-to-Coast Investigations? Three hundred dollars an hour, plus expenses! Someone at the salon found out—"

"So now maybe you can let Tim off from paying that two hundred and thirty-seven ninety-nine," Freddie put in.

"When the case is solved and the money's returned—sure."

"Nice try, Freddie!" said Tim, grinning ruefully.

In a way, it *was* a game Mrs. Kowalski caught them playing. A game for two players, like Power Patrol. Only instead of taking turns to be Driver and Shooter, Freddie was definitely the Drawer and Tim the Measurer.

Tim had been surprised to find out just how good at drawing Freddie was. Felicity herself could hardly have made a better job of the plans and sketches she'd asked them to make. Such as:

(1) the plan of the top of the counter, showing the exact location of the appliances, plus the position of the mysterious heap of brown granules;

(2) the plan of the floor at the foot of the counter, showing the footprints and the other heap of granules there;

(3) the close-up sketch of one of the clearest footprints; and

(4) and (5) a close-up sketch of each of the spilled heaps.

Felicity might have made a *quicker* job of it. Freddie was really taking pains over this.

"We can't afford to mess this up," he said.

Tim couldn't argue with that. Freddie was so enthusiastic he even drew a plan that Felicity hadn't asked for. This one of the complete kitchen—which he said showed what a clear view of Hippo anyone would have had through the window when the lights were on. "A real thief's-eye view!" he'd called it, adding Felicity's sign for a victim clue. Then: "With or without binoculars!" he'd added, in a grim voice.

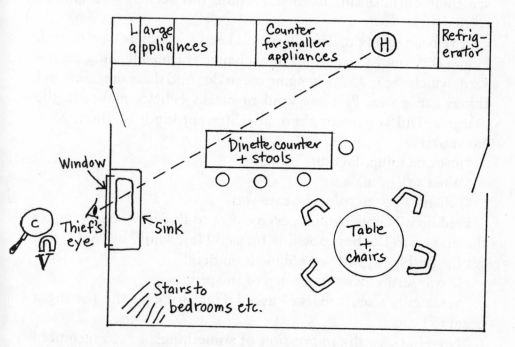

"This light-colored mud," Freddie remarked after a while, "it makes the pattern stand out clearer."

"What pattern?" said Mrs. Kowalski. "It's only that smaller footprint near the door that *has* a pattern. And we know who made *that*!"

"Sure," said Tim. "But Felicity says the fact that the thief's don't have a sole and heel pattern could be the most important clue of all."

"And if there's a mark of any other kind, like a small cut, I should be able to spot it with this," murmured Freddie, bending closer over the magnifying glass.

Mrs. Kowalski herself was very impressed. She helped herself to a Coke and kept out of the way. She was obviously very pleased to see their enthusiasm. Even if Freddie did seem to be getting carried away. . . .

"I've been saying to Tim, we could keep a complete case record. I can get Mom to type it up in exchange for me cleaning up the yard, which she's always bugging me to do. And these diagrams and things can go in. Plus the kind of marks Felicity makes in the margins. Did *you* know there are different kinds of clues, Mrs. Kowalski?"

"Just one thing, Freddie."

"What's that, ma'am?"

"Felicity's got to *solve* the case yet!"

Freddie was now bending even closer to the print, trying to get the glass into the best possible focus. "Hey, Tim!" he said. "Just get the flashlight, will you? Shine it on here!"

He was scrutinizing the instep of the print.

"See a cut, a scuff mark?" asked Tim, bringing the flashlight beam to bear.

"No—but . . . the *impression* of something . . . ," murmured Freddie. Then he stiffened. "Darned if it doesn't look like *printing*! Maybe the brand name!"

14

The Mailman's Clues

"My!" said Felicity, the next morning, when she saw the bunch of papers in Freddie's hand. "You look as if you've been busy!"

"You bet, ma'am!" said Freddie, handing them over.

Tim pointed to the one on top, with the drawings of the piece of unpopped corn.

"This is a brand-new clue we found yesterday when we got back. We think it's a straightforward criminal clue."

"Yeah," said Freddie, "that's why I put the small black mask next to it—see?"

Felicity looked puzzled. "A *molar*?"

"No, ma'am. That's what we thought it was at first. But really . . . "

They explained what had happened when they'd found it, and Freddie's theory of how it had got there.

Felicity looked extremely interested. She nodded with approval at Freddie's demonstration of the perpetrator's eagerness to count the money—the furtive dipping into the bag, his guilty glances to see if anyone was watching.

"Now that could be very useful," said Felicity. "I'll have to give it some more thought. Meanwhile, though—about the clues you'd already found . . . " She turned to the rest of Freddie's drawings and flipped through them eagerly. "You've made a really good job of these footprints," she said. "They're almost as good as photographs."

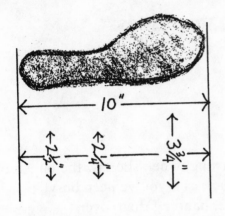

Length of foot = 10"
Width of sole = 3¾"
Width of instep = 2¼"
Width of heel = 2½"

"It was Freddie's idea to color them," said Tim.

"Just a light gray wash mainly," Freddie added. "It gives a better idea of the smoothness of the soles."

"Except for that scrap of writing you spotted on the instep," Tim reminded him, in a low voice.

Felicity didn't seem to be listening. She was still admiring Freddie's artwork.

"Anyway, congratulations, Freddie!" she said. She was looking now at Freddie's sketches of the granules. He'd colored them a light brown with small white highlights that made them seem to glisten. "I like the way you've shown the scattering of the grains— the pattern they made. . . . That's *really* going to help, if they're as accurate as they look."

"Oh, they are, Felicity!" Tim said. "I checked the measurements myself . . . . But *how* will they help? We still can't figure out what they were *doing* there."

"I'll show you." There was a blue jar next to the computer on the counter. Felicity picked it up. It was brimful of the same kind of glistening granules. "Sugar," she said. "I aim to demonstrate—oh, excuse me . . ."

The mailman had just arrived.

"Never mind the sugar!" Freddie whispered. "Let's get her to look at this writing." He pulled a scrap of paper from his pocket. He hadn't even tried to reproduce on the footprint the few letters he'd spotted. They'd been too faint. He'd simply written down the various versions of what he and Tim and Mrs. Kowalski *thought* they looked like.

Felicity was talking to the mailman.

"By the way, Mr. Charles, what time do you usually make deliveries in the Congregational Church neighborhood?"

"*His* neighborhood?" The man nodded at Tim. "Oh, usually around nine, nine fifteen."

"Yesterday, too?"

"Sure. Every—well . . . Maybe a little later yesterday, because of the rain."

"Not as late as ten fifty or eleven, then?"

"No, ma'am. I was already in the Willow Park area at that time. Nice and sunny by then."

"Anyway," said Felicity, "when you *were* in that vicinity, did you notice any strangers hanging around?"

Mr. Charles shook his head. "Didn't notice *no one* hanging around. It was raining hard. Not even any of the people living there."

"Oh?"

"Well, there's usually *someone* around. On the way to the hardware store. In and out the Laundromat. Folks looking in on neighbors." Mr. Charles frowned. "Correction. I tell a lie. I *did* see one person. Only he wasn't exactly *hanging around*."

Felicity looked up sharply. "Who?"

73

"Reverend East. Setting out on his regular jog, with his back-pack to keep his shoulders straight. Every day around that time. Rain or shine."

"Hmm!" murmured Felicity, when Mr. Charles had gone. "That's two *very* interesting points!"

Tim's eyes widened. "*What* two points, Felicity?"

"I'll have to give *them* some more thought, too. . . . But first let's get on with examining the clues we've *already* got." She turned to the counter and picked up the sugar jar. "Pass me the mug, please, Elaine."

15

Felicity's Experiments

Felicity filled the mug with sugar.

By now a small crowd of kids was hovering around, watching her with increasing curiosity. They edged closer. J. G. was among them. He was smirking slightly, as if all this secretly amused him. It made Tim feel uneasy. The jerk can't have been grounded after all! he was thinking. I wonder what he's got up his sleeve?

Freddie, on the other hand, seemed more interested in J. G.'s shoes, judging from the keen glances he kept shooting in that direction. Then Tim realized his friend was chiefly concerned with what size they were and if maybe they had smooth soles with traces of strange lettering on them.

But all at once, Felicity did something that drove these thoughts clean out of Tim's mind, grabbing everyone's full attention and even freezing the lopsided smirk on J. G.'s face.

"Quick! Quick!" she muttered. "Where is it, where is it? . . . Ah, *there* you are!"

She stepped in front of the computer, still clutching the piled-up mug. Then she slammed down the mug and grabbed the computer with both hands.

Then, after lifting the computer a couple of inches, she put it down and turned to Tim and Freddie.

"No, don't look at *me*! Just take a look at *that*!"

She was pointing to the counter just in front of the mug. Some of the sugar had spilled out. It made a small, untidy, crescent-shaped heap like the one they'd found on the Kowalski counter.

"How about *that*?" said Felicity, holding up Freddie's sketch.

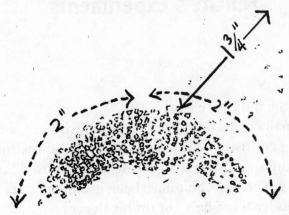

"Hey! Wow!" breathed Tim. "The thief must have been holding a mugful of sugar when—"

"Yeah, but *why*?" said Freddie. "What's a sneak-thief doing, toting a loaded mug of sugar? Pepper, yes. It might have made sense. Ready to throw into someone's face if they caught him in the act. But *sugar* . . . ?"

Felicity was smiling. But she obviously wasn't ready to answer this question.

"Then there's the heap on the floor," she said. "Let's see if we can reconstruct that. But not here. This is carpeted. The pattern of the spill will be different. We need a hard surface, like your kitchen floor. Tiles."

"But with a doormat," added Freddie.

"The lobby!" said Tim.

Felicity was already heading in that direction.

By now the other kids were following her as closely as Tim and Freddie. Most of *them* didn't know what it was all about, of course.

But they had the look of kids to whom nothing that Felicity did, however puzzling, could possibly be of no account.

There was, of course, an exception. One kid *did* seem to know all about it.

J. G. had been watching Felicity's every move, like a teacher watching a bright student performing a difficult procedure. Nodding approval and now and then turning to Holly Jenks with quiet comments. Just occasionally frowning and shaking his head as if to say, "This Snell girl's bright, but she still has a few things to learn."

Tim had been right. Obviously J. G. hadn't been grounded after all. In fact, what had happened was this: John Farrell had managed to win over his father's support yesterday afternoon by telling him of his suspicions about Freddie.

"Yeah," said Mr. Farrell, still steamed up from his encounter with the Fisher girls, "I guess you're onto something this time. This thieving runs in families, all right. I've never forgotten the sneaky way his old man helped himself to some of my slush fund."

"Is that a fact, Dad?" said J. G., his gray eye brightening.

"Yeah. I used to keep my spare change for lunch money, tolls, and stuff in an old cigar box under a pile of oily rags in my cab. It happened when I left it for a coupla minutes, one time when I had to spread sand on a bit of an oil spill on the sidewalk. I'd been making a delivery opposite the Fisher house and that guy must have been watching like a hawk. But I caught him in the act!"

"Yes, Dad!" J. G. murmured soothingly as he popped his father another can of ice-cold beer. "It's a good thing alert detective ability runs in families, too!"

"You bet!" said Mr. Farrell, for once oozing with glowing approval of his only son. "And I hope you nail that Freddie Fisher. I sure do! It'll learn them *all* a lesson. Them sisters of his don't look none too honest, either!"

"Oh, you're right, Dad. You're absolutely right. I'm working on that angle. That Ruth, especially!"

So that's why J. G. looked cockier than ever that morning, strengthened by such unexpected support. He'd even brought along his father's old pipe. He kept furtively pulling it from his pocket to give it a quiet good-luck rub—as if to keep what he'd called the family "alert detective ability" running smoothly.

But Felicity had now reached the library's main door. "Stand back!" she said to the retinue of kids. Still with the mug in her hand, she got hold of the doorknob. Then, without looking at the mug she opened the door. Naturally, the doorknob turned, the mug turned with it and some of the sugar was spilled onto the mat and the tiles.

"Don't forget, I'm the sneak-thief. I'm too busy looking to see if anyone's likely to see me coming out. Now," she crouched down, "let's see what pattern *this* made."

She'd brought along Freddie's other sugar-spill sketch.

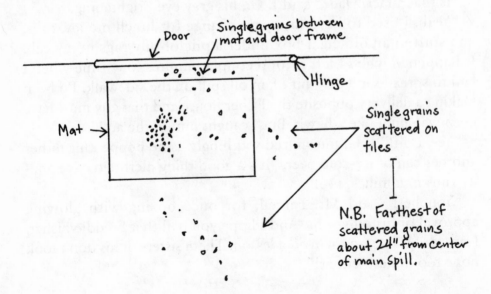

78

Tim and Freddie and most of the other kids crouched with her. "There, you see," she said. "Very similar once again."

"But, of course!" J. G. murmured to Holly Jenks. "What did she expect?"

Then they all jumped as a voice boomed out:

"Hey, youse pilgrims! What you think you're doin'? If . . . Oh—uh—sorry, Ms. Snell! Didn't see you was there. . . ."

It was the janitor. He'd been stalking the kids ever since he'd noticed one of them pulling a pipe from his pocket. He'd been thinking, Let him just dare! Just let him try lighting it in my library!

But now, seeing the librarian sprinkle that stuff on his nice clean floor had driven all that from his mind.

Slowly, Felicity arose and, smiling sweetly, said, "I'm sorry, Mr. Snerdoff. I was just running an urgent experiment. But you won't need your mop. A vacuum will be all for getting the granules up."

"Granules?"

"Yes. But it's okay. It's only sugar."

Ernest Snerdoff looked relieved.

"No problem, Ms. Snell. Not like the paint on the rug in there last week, huh?"

"No, thank goodness! I'm *still* sorry about that!"

"Yeah, well," said the janitor. "These things happen."

When they went back into the junior room, Felicity explained to Tim and Freddie, "He was in a terrible state about that paint, poor guy! The carpeting in here's less than six months old. It's his pride and joy—"

"What happened?"

"I'd been working on a picture of a red dragon with some of the little kids. Part of a storytelling session. Then someone knocked over the red poster paint."

79

The Fisher girls and most of the other younger kids were all listening openly now, as if *this* was a story session. They obviously remembered the incident very clearly, grinning and nodding. Even J. G. seemed to have fallen under the spell.

"Oh, boy!" groaned Freddie, looking down at the light pearly gray carpet.

"Yeah!" said Felicity. She dropped her voice and addressed Tim and Freddie alone. "Mr. Snerdoff was on his knees fussing with it for over an hour. That's when I heard about his Purple Heart. He said the paint reminded him of the blood that was all over the inside of a burning gunship when he was rescuing the crew. And the rest of the story came out while he fussed over the carpet. Anxiety does that to some people. Loosens their tongue so they hardly know what they're saying. I guess when the mind's grappling with a crisis, the mouth gets to blabber unchecked."

"Yes, my mom's like that," said Tim. "When she has a problem with someone's hair. Like you noticed yourself . . ."

"About all those personal details that came out about *you*? Yes. Of course." Felicity was looking *very* thoughtful now. "I'm glad you reminded me." Felicity became businesslike again. "But didn't I hear you saying something about some writing on one of the footprints?" She picked up the sketches and frowned. "I don't see any writing here."

"No," said Freddie. "That's because we weren't sure exactly which letters they were. They were so faint and patchy." He brought out the extra sheet. "So I wrote them on here. What we could make out."

Felicity frowned at the shadowy letters. J. G. edged forward. He, too, frowned. Maybe worried, thought Tim.

"We figured an *e* and a *w* with a couple more *e*'s underneath," said Freddie.

"And something with an upstroke in front of the bottom two," said Tim. "Like it might have been part of a *b* or *f* or *h*."

"Also, I couldn't be *really* sure about those *e*'s," said Freddie. "Some might have been *o*'s. I thought at first it might be what was left of the words *new boots*."

"And my mom thought it might be part of the words *cowboy boots*!" said Tim. "It just didn't make any sense! Any of it."

Apparently, it didn't make sense to J. G., either. His frown had deepened.

So did the frowns of the other onlookers, who were crowding closer again.

"Of course not," said Felicity. "You were looking at it all wrong!"

She went behind the counter and fished her purse out of a drawer. "Whatever letters and words were stamped on the instep must have been reversed in the prints."

Suddenly, J. G.'s frown disappeared—to be replaced by that superior smile. As if he was saying, "Well, *of course*! I could have told you *that*!"

Felicity took a small mirror from the purse. "Now, let's see what we've got."

They stared at the reverse image of Freddie's letters.

"Those bottom ones are o's, I think," Felicity murmured. "But I'd have to see the prints myself."

"*Wet wool?*" Freddie was grinning.

"That last letter could be incomplete," said Felicity. "It could be part of a *b* or *t* or—"

"*Wet foot?*" said Freddie, still grinning.

J. G. could no longer resist it.

"No, wait!" he said. "All of you. How about Wet Boot? Huh?" He gave Freddie a keen, searching look, his gray eye glittering. Then the brown one seemed to take over, glowing with enthusiasm, as he looked around at the audience, including Felicity, Holly Jenks, Spencer Curtis, Freddie's sisters, and all the other kids who were listening and watching. "I think the time has come," he said, "to unmask the real perpetrator!"

16

J. G.'s Two-Pipe Problem

There was a stunned silence.

"Go on!" murmured Felicity, looking impressed.

She'd heard all about J. G. About how he thought he was such a great detective. About his wild, wild imagination. About how most kids thought he was a screwball. She'd seen him hovering that morning, taking everything in, looking so very superior. Just as she'd been perfectly aware of his antics the day before, snooping on her conversation with Tim and Freddie, dying to know details of the theft, busting to get a look at the notes she'd made. She was also aware of how he'd been getting kids like Holly Jenks and Spencer Curtis to snoop for him.

She didn't mind all that. She knew that anyone who had ambitions to be a detective couldn't help being curious. She knew that healthy curiosity was one of a detective's most valuable assets. She even had a soft spot for those who let their imaginations run away with them. They usually ran straight into trouble, made false deductions, and, even worse, false accusations. But sometimes their wild imaginations hit on a key fact. Then a *really* good detective, in charge of such screwballs, could make valuable use of it.

And here, she told herself, in J. G. Farrell we have a Screwball Supreme!

She smiled encouragingly. "Go on, John. Let us hear your theory."

She'd had to tell him this a second time, because for a minute or two he'd seemed to be hesitating.

Not from uncertainty, though. Not J. G. Farrell!

That kid was never uncertain about anything that had found its way into his dark crew-cut head.

He was simply hesitating until he arranged his ideas—ideas about how to show off his talents to the best advantage.

"Thank you, Ms. Snell," he said, at last. "I was wondering when you'd get around to calling me in."

Then there was a gasp from the others as he pulled out a pipe and began to pace back and forth in front of the counter. Even Felicity looked taken aback.

"You aren't thinking of *smoking* that, are you?" she said.

Already Ernest Snerdoff was looking in at the door, eyes popping.

J. G. looked startled, then sheepish.

"Uh—no, ma'am. It's my dad's. It gives me inspiration. Like Sherlock Holmes when he was thinking about a case. Like he'd say, 'This is a three-pipe problem.' Meaning he'd smoke three pipes before he solved it. Now *this* would only be a two-pipe problem to him, I guess. Also to me. Only, of course, I don't actually smoke it. I just hold it.

"Anyway, talking about smoking," he continued, "all this sugar and footprints and stuff *is* just smoke." He pointed to his copy of Felicity's notes. "Just one big smoke screen. Planted by the perpetrators to put people like us off the trail. You're wasting your time, Ms. Snell. Red herring stuff. What *you'd* call a bunch of *phantom* clues, I guess."

Most of the other kids were now silent, astounded at this challenge to their heroine. Even Tim and Freddie were wondering what was coming next. Felicity herself was merely looking politely curious.

"Go on, John," she murmured again.

"It all points to one person as the mastermind," he said, looking straight at Freddie. "And he knows who he is!"

"Just because of my father—!" Freddie blurted out.

"No," said J. G., shaking his head and smiling that know-it-all smile. "Even if your father had been president of the United States, the facts would still point to *you*."

He leveled the pipe at Freddie like a gun. Freddie growled.

"You're just a screwball!" he retorted. "Even if your mother had been an Arabian princess like you once said, you'd still be a screwball!"

J. G. ignored the jibe. He shrugged his shoulders and broadened that maddening grin.

Freddie was getting fit to be tied by now, as Tim could tell. So were Freddie's sisters, judging from the looks on their faces. Felicity must have thought so, too. She stepped in with a second note of calm. "Go on, John. I'm still listening. What are the *facts*?"

With this encouragement, J. G. relaxed even more. He hitched himself into a sitting position on the counter—high above everyone else. It was where Felicity herself sometimes sat when reading a story to the older kids. With the pipe cradled in one hand, holding it close to his chest, he looked the picture of the great detective about to spill the beans. His right eye was screwed up shrewdly as if peering into every corner of all that had taken place. His left eye now glowed warmly, enjoying this sense of power.

"Well," he began, "first you must realize there are three things every detective must look for. The means, the motive, and the opportunity. Did the suspect have the *means* to commit the crime? Did he have a *motive*? Did he have the *opportunity*? The person I am about to unmask fits all three, right up to the hilt. . . ." He lowered his voice. "Holly, Spencer—stand near the door in case he tries to make a break for it."

Holly Jenks and Spencer Curtis looked at each other and edged closer to the door, glancing uneasily at Freddie. No doubt J. G. was thinking of all the mysteries on TV where the unmasked killer shouts, "You'll never take me alive!" and goes crashing through the window.

But no one looked less likely than Freddie to do anything so desperate. He was just staring at J. G. as if the kid had gone completely nuts.

"The facts, John," Felicity urged.

"Well, number one, as to opportunity," said J. G. "You were *there*, Freddie Fisher. On the spot. You were there when the corn popper and the money were stolen."

"So what?" said Tim, stoutly backing his friend. "So was I. I was also on the spot, wasn't I? I mean—I—I *live* there for Pete's sake!"

"Sure!" said J. G. almost triumphantly. "And that doesn't let you off the hook, either. . . . I'll be coming to that. . . . But now as to motive."

"Yeah, what motive?" said Ruth. She was beginning to look mad, too.

"The money, of course," said J. G. "As if you didn't know! The two thousand dollars plus, stashed in the corn popper."

"You're not even right about that!" said Tim. "It was nowhere near that much!"

Felicity was nodding. "Tim's right, John. But put that aside for the time being. How do you reckon Freddie could get the money and the corn popper away from the house, from under Tim's nose, without him noticing?"

J. G. simply smirked, totally unfazed.

"Well, if they were in it together, there'd *be* no problem, would there, ma'am?"

Tim felt his face burn with anger. "Of all the—," he began. Felicity gripped his arm.

"Let's assume that Tim had nothing to do with it," she said. "How could Freddie have managed it on his own?"

J. G. still stayed cool. (Would *nothing* wipe that smirk off his face? Tim was beginning to wonder.)

"By the clever use of outside accomplices, ma'am. And false footprints."

"*What* outside accomplices?" Freddie burst out. "The Reverend East? Mr. Charles the mailman? Batman and Robin?"

J. G. simply made himself more comfortable, leaning back on one elbow on the counter.

"How about your sister Ruth for starters?" he said. "And maybe the others as well? All in it together. Yeah, including Robyn with a *y* if it comes to that. The *whole* family!"

"You'll be saying my father was in it next!" said Freddie bitterly.

This was received with a kind of gloating joy.

"Oh, he was! He was!" crowed J. G. "In a way."

It might have been that tone of voice that proved to be the last straw. For the previous few minutes Julie, Robyn, and Ruth had been whispering together, the two younger ones getting madder and madder by the look of them, with Ruth trying to calm them. But when J. G. said that about their father being involved, there was no holding them.

"Right!" said Julie. "That's it! I'm not standing for this, John Farrell! Let's do it, Robyn!"

"Sure thing!" said Robyn, a gleeful light in her eye.

"No!" said Ruth. "Stop!"

But before Ruth or Felicity could prevent them, they'd darted to the counter and each had grabbed one of J. G.'s legs and yanked it upward.

After that it was pure pandemonium for a few seconds.

17

J. G. Builds Up His Case

J. G. had been hugely enjoying playing the part of the great detective. To have his audience hanging on every word—including Felicity herself!—to have the true perpetrators squirm as he got closer to revealing their secrets—all this gave him a great feeling of power. Enjoying it? He'd been *relishing* it.

Which was why he'd allowed himself to relax and get *too* comfortable, so that when the two girls made their sudden move he was taken completely off his guard.

He felt his ankles being grabbed. He felt his feet being jerked upward. And he could do nothing about it!

He found himself falling backward with nothing to grab hold of except his pipe, which he waved feebly in the air as he went, like a swimmer being carried under by the tide. Luckily there was a life-guard at hand. He might have gone clean over the counter if Elaine hadn't reached out to steady him from behind.

Another person had rushed forward at the same time. But not to the rescue.

This was Freddie.

Tim thought at first his friend had gone to help Ruth quell the two younger ones. But that wasn't necessary, because by then the kids had been so shocked by the unexpected result of their action that they'd frozen in horror. Robyn was already beginning to cry.

But Freddie went straight past them, anyway, and was grabbing J. G.'s ankles for himself.

Not to cause more mayhem, though, but to steady them, so he could get a closer look at the soles of J. G.'s shoes. Which he did. Then he sighed heavily and shook his head.

"They're smooth leather soles, all right," he told Tim, "and about the same size as the footprints. They're the same shoes he was wearing yesterday, too. I recognized the odd strings. One brown, the other gray. Like his eyes. But they've got rubber heels with patterns and rubber tips at the toes. So there was no point in looking for the writing. Those weren't *his* prints in your kitchen. He's in the clear. The jerk!"

Freddie spoke so regretfully that Tim stared. "Don't tell me you *organized* this! That you got those kids to do this deliberately so you could get a good look at his footwear!"

By now Ruth was apologizing to the badly shaken J. G. and looking almost as shaken herself, and Robyn's tears were being dried by Felicity.

"No, it wasn't like that." A strange smile, part rueful, part proud, crossed Freddie's face. "No need to organize anything with that bunch! They see a guy's in trouble, they want to help. Then when they see a way of doing it—*wham!*—they jump at the chance. No questions. No discussion. They just do it. We're like that in our family!"

Yeah, gun-jumpers yourselves! thought Tim.

It turned out later that Freddie had gone home the evening before, full of his discovery of some kind of writing on the footprints. Also full of his conviction that J. G. Farrell was the sneak-thief.

The girls hadn't said much but they'd certainly taken it to heart. Julie had even mentioned the golden opportunity they'd missed near the fishpond, when J. G. had been sitting on the backrest of the bench, with his shoes only an inch or two from their noses.

"But we didn't know about the writing on the footprints *then*," Ruth had reminded them.

Well, now they did, and they'd been given a second chance. With J. G. perched on the counter of the junior library, shooting his mouth off. Trying to get their brother blamed. Dropping their father's name into it. And those shoes only inches away from their noses *again*!

"We just had to go for it this time!" said Julie.

"And we didn't mean to *hurt* him!" said Robyn. "We didn't know he'd go toppling over backward."

"Just to get a look at those shoe soles is all we wanted," said Julie.

So who could blame them?

Felicity Snell didn't, anyway.

She soon saw there'd been no real malice, and nothing harmed except J. G.'s feelings.

"You all right, John?" she said.

"Yes—uh—sure, ma'am."

"Good! So just carry on with your interesting theory. The facts. And how you think they prove that someone in the house could have spirited the popper and the money away. Using outside accomplices. And what the words *Wet Boots* have got to do with it. . . . And—uh—you should *stand* in front of the counter, this time."

J. G. took her advice. He was no longer comfortable. He was still looking pale and shaken. He looked as if he was glad to keep his feet firmly on the carpet. His smirk had faded. And the pipe had been pushed back in his pocket.

But the guy was still game. Tim had to give him that!

"Well, I know *she* was in the vicinity." He gave Ruth a dirty look. "I saw her myself. Close to the Kowalski house. And she was carrying a bag."

"It was a *laundry* bag!" Ruth protested indignantly. "I was on my way to the Laundromat."

"Sure!" said J. G., the smirk beginning to twitch his lips again. "A really clever cover story! With the bag ready to slip the popper into as well as—"

"What d'you *mean*, 'slip the popper into'?" Freddie fairly howled, getting mad again. "You saying she hung around outside and whistled for Hippo like a dog. So he'd come trotting out and give himself up, complete with the money?"

The smirk came back in full. With an infuriating "*tsk!*" J. G. turned to Felicity and said, "Isn't it always the same! The way they get mad and start to bluster when they're confronted by the truth?"

Felicity refused to take sides.

"Just answer his question, John. What d'you *think* Ruth was going to do with the bag?"

J. G. turned to Freddie as he answered.

"Walk straight into the kitchen with it, the way *you*, Freddie Fisher, had arranged—while you kept Tim busy upstairs. I bet you turned up the volume at that point, so it would cover any noise downstairs."

He glanced back at the counter. He was getting comfortable again. Felicity was quick to keep him where he was.

"And the footprints?" she said, shoving Freddie's drawing and Tim's measurements under his nose. "Ten inches long?" Then she pointed to Ruth's feet. "They're nowhere *near* that."

"Well," said J. G., full of confidence again, "that's what the words *Wet Boots* put me in mind of. Like they were maybe the brand name of some kind of overshoes."

Felicity nodded. "Good point," she murmured. "Go on."

"So that's how it was done," said J. G., pulling out his pipe and stabbing it in Ruth's direction. "She had taken the precaution of slipping on a pair of overshoes several sizes too large. Probably a pair her father had left behind. That's what I meant about *him* being an accomplice, too, in a way."

Everyone was silent again. Even Tim couldn't help feeling that this seemed to be making sense.

Could there have been some truth in it?

He glanced at Freddie. His friend's face had darkened a deep red. So had Ruth's. Just plain anger again? Or *guilt*?

18

Felicity Shoots It Down

Felicity was holding Robyn closer and keeping her other hand on Julie. She shook her head.

"That's just where your theory breaks down, John. But go on. Let's think it through, step by step. . . . The accomplice has walked in in her oversize overshoes—what next?"

"She goes straight to Hippo, sweeps him off the counter into the bag, goes back to the door, takes off the overshoes, and puts them in the bag, too. Then she goes out, closing the door behind her—mission accomplished. Anyone seeing her coming out thinks nothing of it. Just some kid running an errand to the Laundromat. But no one does happen to be watching. Except me. And even *I* was fooled at the time. So she calmly walks away with both loot and boots, removing all the evidence from the scene of the crime. A very clever plan that only someone with a cunning inborn criminal mind could have dreamed up."

"Or someone with a vivid imagination and a poor feeling for accuracy," said Felicity, coolly, before the growl that had risen in Freddie's throat could burst out in a full-blown roar.

Felicity's remark had pulled up J. G. just as effectively.

His smirk had faded again.

"Ma'am?" he faltered.

"Yes, because look—" Felicity had reached for her pad and

started drawing—"your whole theory hangs on the use of over-shoes, right?"

"Yes, ma'am. . . ." The gray and the brown eye began crossing as J. G. watched the drawing take shape.

"Well, it was a good idea," murmured Felicity, with the other kids beginning to crowd around. "But it doesn't account for that smoothness of the actual footprints. You weren't to know, of course," she added, smiling sweetly. "You didn't make a routine close inspection of the prints, like a really careful professional detective. But that smoothness, that lack of pattern would have ruled out overshoes right away. Galoshes, overshoes, are for wet or slushy weather, when the ground's slick. They *always* have deep patterns on the soles and heels. To get a better grip."

She held up her now completed sketch. "Like this . . . ."

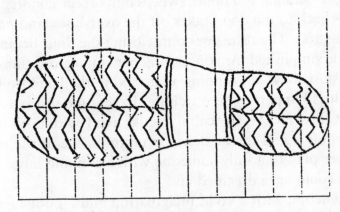

J. G. was now completely silenced. His mouth opened but nothing came out. Then it shut. Then opened again. Still no comment. Like a fish gasping for air.

Then the clapping started, led by Ruth herself.

"Yeah!" she jeered. "How about *that*, Mister Big Detective?"

Again J. G.'s mouth opened and shut, but more slowly, as if he kept getting the *start* of an idea, only to think better of it. No one had ever seen J. G. looking so totally fazed.

But he wasn't finished yet. Not that guy!

Gradually the brown eye opened fully. And when it did it was glowing.

"All right," he said. "So it wasn't overshoes. But she could have used a pair of old bedroom slippers. Her mother's maybe. And I bet she did!"

It was J. G.'s one last jump of the gun and he was giving it all he'd got.

Felicity was looking interested.

"Yes," she murmured. "I suppose she could at that. . . ."

Out came the smirk again and the cocky superior look.

But Felicity had started sketching again, this time adding strokes to Freddie's drawing of the firm, smooth-soled footprints.

"But then, you see, John, the prints would have come out like *this*, with Ruth slithering and slipping about as she tried to keep the slippers on her feet."

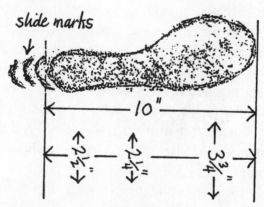

There was a murmur from the watching kids. Those of them with younger sisters who liked dressing up in their mom's shoes

95

knew exactly what Felicity was getting at. Freddie, with *three* younger sisters, was beaming broadly.

But J. G. still wasn't licked. . . .

"Well—uh—I see what you mean, ma'am," he faltered. *"However . . ."* The brown eye was glowing again as he turned to Julie. "It could have been *her,* not Ruth. Walking on her hands like she's good at. With her hands keeping a firm grip on the slippers."

"Sure," said Julie, suddenly enthusiastic despite just having been nominated the new prime suspect. "I *could* do that. If I spread my fingers so they gripped the sides of the slippers. They wouldn't slither about *then.*"

J. G. pounced.

"Let's see you do it then!" He turned to Felicity. "Why don't you let her demonstrate, Ms. Snell? Using your sneakers?"

Felicity, always keen to try a new experiment, was already taking them off.

"Sure. Go ahead, Julie."

Julie needed no further invitation. She was standing on her hands even as Felicity was speaking, fired by the honor of actually walking in Felicity's footsteps—and upside down at that!

Only Tim and Freddie seemed to have realized that this wasn't doing Freddie's case a whole bundle of good. As Julie took three or four steps, keeping her fingers stretched wide inside Felicity's sneakers, proving the jerk's point for him that she could have left perfect footprints using her mother's slippers, Freddie burst out: "Oh sure! So how could she swipe Hippo if she was using her hands for *walking?*"

J. G. was ready for him—one jump ahead as ever.

"She could have picked it up with her *feet,* that's how. Right, Ms. Snell?"

Felicity looked doubtful.

96

"There was a female contortionist and acrobat at a circus I once worked at. *She* could do wonderful things with her feet. She had very flexible toes, like fingers. She could use them better than most people use their hands. But *she* was a professional—"

"So could I!" said Julie. "Let me try, Felicity. Give me something to try it on."

Still upside down she was already wriggling out of her own sneakers, freeing her toes for the challenge.

Felicity hesitated, probably fearing the experiment was getting out of hand.

But J. G. had no such doubts.

"Sure, why not?" He drew the sugar jar closer to the edge of the counter. "Imagine this is Hippo."

Julie tried valiantly. Ernest Snerdoff could have called her "pilgrim" with some justification right then. With her hands in Felicity's sneakers she moved up to the counter and turned, with the rest of her body arching over the jar.

19

J. G.'s New Assignment?

Everyone watched in total silence. Her brother, Freddie, was hoping she'd fail. Her accuser, J. G., was hoping she'd succeed and prove his point. Tim couldn't make up his mind, but he was fascinated all the same.

Julie's right foot touched the rim of the jar.

Unfortunately, her toes were *not* as flexible as fingers.

But she didn't give in. She still kept trying, this time with both feet. No nonsense about using her toes, either! She gripped the jar firmly between her feet and slowly lifted it clear of the counter.

There was another burst of applause.

"Way to go!" said J. G.

"Yeah!" growled Freddie. "Now let's see you carry it as far as the *door* like that. Still walking on your hands!"

Julie seemed to have lost all sense of whose side she was on. Reveling in the applause, spurred by J. G.'s encouragement, she headed back alongside the counter, the jar wavering between her feet, concentrating on keeping her grip on it—*and* Felicity's sneakers firmly on her hands. She'd reckoned on going as far as the computer to represent the Kowalski kitchen door, like six or seven steps, say. With J. G. (the kid she'd nearly sent flying off balance only half an hour ago!) hovering at her side, ready to lend a steadying hand, she began her precarious journey.

But she never made it.

Four steps turned out to be her limit. Past the fuming Freddie. Past Tim. Past her sister Ruth. Then the jar slipped. She made a brave attempt to stop it by squeezing harder with her feet, but the movement only succeeded in giving the jar a kick. It crashed to the carpet at J. G.'s feet, not breaking but scattering sugar all over the place.

"Hey!" came the roar from the entrance.

"It's all right, Mr. Snerdoff!" said Felicity, retrieving her sneakers. "It's still only sugar." She turned to J. G. "So you see, John, your theory just doesn't stand up in practice, does it?"

"Neither did Julie," said Ruth, with a mysterious smile. "But don't look so miffed, honey. It proves you didn't do what John Farrell was saying. You couldn't do the trick, maybe. But you couldn't have swiped the popper, either!"

Julie brightened a little.

"No. I hadn't thought of that. . . . But I *might* have done it if somebody hadn't blowed on my bare toes just then and tickled them."

"Probably just a draft," said Ruth, looking solemn behind her glasses. "I mean who would play a trick like that?"

Julie shook her head, but Tim thought *he* knew who.

Someone who stayed cool enough to remember whose side *she* was on! *That* was who!

Meanwhile, J. G. was still looking dismayed. He sighed deeply. "I guess I *was* kind of reaching," he murmured.

Strangely enough, that reluctant admission made a much stronger impression on the listeners than all his cocky Big Detective bluster earlier.

Maybe he's not such a jerk, after all, Tim was thinking.

"Well, you can't win 'em all," was Ruth's comment.

Even Freddie was beginning to look at him with a slightly less hostile glint in his eyes.

And Felicity herself was smiling with open sympathy.

"Well, cheer up, John," she said. "Your experiment *was* successful, in a way. It proved that Julie or Ruth couldn't have made those footprints using overshoes or large slippers. But it *has* given me a good idea of what actually did happen. Your input could have created the big breakthrough we needed."

J. G. looked dazed. "It—it *could*?"

"Yes," said Felicity. She turned to Tim and Freddie. "Why don't I stop by at the scene of the crime and take a look at the actual footprints myself?"

"When?" asked Freddie.

"As soon as possible after I've made a few inquiries. I happen to know exactly where we can find out about different brand names of footwear."

"Great!" said Tim. "Uh—what time d'you think—?"

"Say eleven forty-five," said Felicity. "And while you're waiting, you can be making a sketch-map of your immediate neighborhood. Showing those houses you can see from your own back doorstep. Or, more importantly, where people can see *your* house from *their* places."

"You still haven't told us why the sneak-thief was going around with a mug of sugar," Freddie reminded her as she picked up the now empty jar and replaced it on the counter.

"I know," said Felicity. "I'm not *quite* sure myself yet. I think John Farrell might have hit on it with something he said. But it's all beginning to tie in. The sugar. The footprints. The timetable. The weather. A good map of the neighborhood might just clinch it. So get onto it right away and I'll see you in"—she glanced at her watch—"fifty minutes."

As they were about to move away she turned to J. G.

"You stay here, John. There's something I want to discuss with you. You girls, too," she added, nodding at Ruth, Julie, and Robyn.

J. G. looked puzzled, but brightened at the tone of the invitation. Somehow Felicity had made it sound like a police chief's calling on the FBI for their expert advice and assistance. The three Fisher girls looked wildly delighted at the prospect whatever it was, even though they, too, were just as much in the dark.

Tim and Freddie wondered what Felicity had in mind.

"You think she believed the jerk after all?" Freddie said as they hurried down the library steps. "That we *did* have something to do with it?"

"Or she *suspects* him and is holding him for further questioning?" said Tim. "All that interest in who can see our house from theirs?"

"Well, that puts *him* in the frame for sure," said Freddie.

"But, no," said Tim after giving this a few moments' thought. "She seemed to be thinking of giving him an assignment. The kids, too."

"Huh!" grunted Freddie. Then he suddenly grinned. "Oh, well! So long as it keeps him and them out of our hair. . . ."

20

Felicity's Emergency Kit

Fifty minutes later there was a knock at the door back at Tim's house and Felicity was standing there. She was looking around—at the yard, the path, the dirt road outside, and the other houses. She was carrying a pink cosmetic case.

"What's *he* doing here?" asked Freddie, sounding very suspicious.

He was looking at the hovering figure of J. G. at the end of the path. Still looking subdued. Not at all his usual cocky self.

"An extra pair of eyes," said Felicity. "An extra half-dozen pairs of eyes, in fact. Since he lives on the spot and knows the neighborhood well, I'm putting him in charge of the Fingertip Search Squad." She turned to Tim. "Now show me exactly where you found the piece of unpopped corn."

"The Fingertip Search Squad?" said Tim, puzzled, as he led the way.

"Yeah!" J. G. piped up. "Very special. Needle-in-haystack kind of search. Needs very skilled organizing, right, Ms. Snell?"

"Oh, yes," said Felicity. "That's why I put you in charge."

"And I'm getting it together," said J. G. "As soon as the others have had their lunch, we'll be onto it. Including a sniffer dog," he added proudly. "My idea. . . . Oh, and your sister Julie, Freddie. She'll be a natural. Also my idea."

Freddie still frowned suspiciously.

"Looking for *what*?"

"Clues of course," said J. G. "Bits of popcorn for a start—right, Felicity?"

"Yes." Felicity turned to Tim who was still gaping at J. G. and wondering what kind of sniffer dog he had in mind. "You haven't told me yet exactly where you found that piece."

"Sorry!" Tim bent down. "Right here."

"This is where you could begin, John," said Felicity. "When the squad's all set and the—uh—sniffer dog arrives. See if there are any more pieces in this vicinity, maybe in the grass or in the road."

J. G. looked slightly puzzled.

"I still don't see what the popcorn was doing here, anyway."

Felicity explained Freddie's theory of the perpetrator's eagerness to check the roll of bills.

"It's a long shot," she said. "But he, or she, might have gone on checking. And if any more pieces were dropped in the same way it could lead us to —"

"But why would they *keep* checking?" asked J. G., his gray eye sharply glinting.

"Because," said Freddie darkly, "he'd been expecting two grand and from the size of the roll there only seemed to be a tenth of that!"

"Yes," said Felicity. "So he or she would be tempted to keep on checking to see if there were some twenties or fifties among those bills."

"But why not wait until he was safely home?" said J. G.

"Because he or she was miffed and rattled," said Felicity.

"Impatient," said Tim. "And greedy."

"Wouldn't *you* be?" said Freddie, in that dark tone again, giving J. G. a look to match it.

"Anyway," said Felicity, "it is a long shot. There's no point in trying to cover this whole area for pieces of popcorn that may not even be there. The main thing is to keep the eyes peeled for where he or she might have got rid of the corn popper itself in the long grass or weeds or undergrowth. There's plenty of *that* around."

"Sure is," murmured J. G., looking less gung ho. Then he brightened. "Excuse me, Ms. Snell. I'd better give the dog handler a call. Remind him not to feed the mutt at lunch. Keep it nice and hungry. On its toes."

"What dog handler?" said Tim. But J. G. was already on his way back to his house. Tim shrugged. "Screwball!" he muttered, shaking his head.

"If *I* was in charge of the search squad," Freddie murmured, watching J. G. go, "I'd stick to the path leading up *there*. But I bet *he* doesn't. Especially if there *is* a sniffer dog."

"Anyway," said Felicity, "I'm here to examine the footprints in your kitchen, Tim."

Tim led the way back to the house and held open the door for her. Before coming in, she inspected the underside of her shoes. There had been some light showers overnight and the path was still rather muddy.

"It's okay to use *this* mat, Felicity," said Tim.

His mother had put it down at the side of the original one, which still displayed its scattering of granules.

As Felicity wiped her feet, she looked down at an upturned cardboard box. It had been placed over the first and clearest of the intruder footprints, and labeled in red:

KEEP CLEAR
DO NOT DISTURB
VITAL EVIDENCE!!

Felicity bent to it. "Is this the one with the writing on it?"

Tim nodded.

"I'm glad to see you know how to preserve the scene of a crime." Felicity glanced across at the counter. They'd used two upturned plastic containers here. "Is that where the first heap of sugar is?"

"If it *is* sugar," said Tim.

"I'll get to that when I've examined this footprint," said Felicity.

She put the cosmetic case on the dinette counter. Then she lifted the cardboard box.

"Hmm!" She gazed down at the light gray print. "It must be pretty dried up by now."

She went and opened the cosmetic case. From that moment, both boys forgot all about J. G. and the Fingertip Search Squad.

The first thing they saw was the makeup palette with its brushes and tweezers and things in slots, and the colors in small round wells. Tim averted his eyes. His mother had once told him it wasn't polite to peer into women's cosmetic cases.

Freddie hadn't been so strictly trained. Tim saw his friend's eyes widen as Felicity rummaged about, lifting up the top compartment and diving into the second layer. Then Tim just couldn't resist a quick peek himself. There was something different about that makeup palette.

It seemed to him to have a very strange selection of colors. Also, the wigs Felicity tossed to one side looked rather weird. Dirty gray, faded red, streaky black.

Felicity must have seen Tim's perplexity.

"Simple disguise kit. *Actor's* makeup, not beautician's. Plus other stuff I used when I worked for Coast-to-Coast. This was my undercover emergency case. Just a harmless vanity case on the outside."

Freddie was goggling.

"Does it carry listening devices, and midget transmitters, and—and *guns*?"

Felicity didn't seem to hear.

She had found what she required: a magnifying glass smaller than the one she'd lent them but which Tim guessed had a much stronger lens, a compact flashlight, and what looked like a small perfume spray.

She placed them on the counter and selected the spray. "This isn't for making anyone smell pretty," she said.

"Is it *mace*?" asked Freddie.

"No. But stand well clear and try not to breathe deeply until it disperses. It only takes a couple of seconds." She kneeled at the side of the box, removed it, and very gently directed a cloud of spray at the print. "Powerful setting solution," she murmured, holding her head well to one side. "Firms up the print without disturbing it any. So it doesn't crumble and lose its marks while I'm examining it."

Then she bent closer with the magnifying glass and spotlight.

"Now let's see if we can make any more sense of this writing. . . ."

21

Felicity Issues More Instructions

The flashlight was brighter than the one Freddie and Tim had used. But despite that, it didn't seem to be making Felicity's task much easier. Occasionally, she'd murmur, "Ah, yes!" and jot something on the pad. But there were also silent spells when she simply moved the glass from one part of the footprint to another and changed the angle of the light or of her head. Once, she murmured, "Very curious!" and then, "Certainly not the kind of footwear you'd expect!" Finally, she stood up.

"We've made a slight advance, anyway. It looks like we might now have *this*."

	c we
	x
	bootexxx

"I've already allowed for the letters being reversed. So what you see is what's actually imprinted on the footwear."

"What are the crosses for?" asked Tim.

"Well, I'm not sure. That first *c*, for instance, could be an *o*. But the *b* is definite. So is the *t* and the *e*. Then there seem to be three more letters, just too faint to be identified."

"Could it be the name of a store?" asked Freddie. *"Owen's boo-tique?"*

"There isn't even the faintest trace of an *n* or *s*. And you don't spell *boutique* with two *o*'s, Freddie."

"What *does* it say, then?"

"Beats me! But the fax I'm expecting this afternoon should make everything clear."

Felicity was crossing her fingers. "By the way," Tim said. "You mentioned something about not the kind of footwear you'd expect. *What* kind, Felicity?"

"Well, that's something else I'm hoping the fax will clear up. . . . Now—about this stuff that was spilled. . . ."

She went to the counter and lifted the upturned containers.

"Oh, yes," she said. "That's sugar, all right. The kind I used this morning. Large-grain Demerara." She took up a pinch and rolled it between finger and thumb. "Feels like it." She put the pinch close to her nose. "Smells like it."

"Also *tastes* like it?" said Freddie, itching to try.

"Hey, no!" gasped Tim. "It could be—"

"Why not?" Felicity touched the pinch with the very tip of her tongue. "Yes, sugar . . . ."

Tim stared. But Felicity didn't turn a bad color, or foam at the mouth, or fall to the floor writhing in agony. Instead, she winked.

"It's okay, Tim. We're not dealing with a mad poisoner. That kind of person would have doctored some of the food in the refrigerator. He or she wouldn't have scattered the deadly crystals in heaps all over the kitchen. Besides, there are all the other signs that he or she was carrying it in a mug or cup quite openly, as if wanting to *advertise* it." She bent to the pad and put a check mark after the query, *sugar*? Then this in the margin:

Tim blinked. "A *phantom* clue, Felicity?"

She was looking at her watch. "I'll explain later." She put her stuff back in the case. "Now—did you make that sketch-map?"

"Yes, *ma'am*!" Freddie handed her the map.

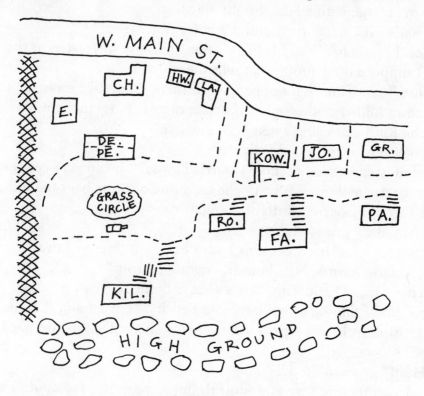

KEY:

KOW.	=	Kowalski house
JO.	=	Jones "
GR.	=	Grant "
PA.	=	Pallance "
FA.	=	Farrell "
RO.	=	Rossi "
KIL.	=	Kilkinder "

CH.	=	Church
E.	=	East house
DE.	=	Dempsey apt.
PE.	=	Peters apt.
HW.	=	Hardware store
LA.	=	Laundromat

"Just what I needed," said Felicity. She took it to the door and looked around outside, checking the details: the other houses, church, hardware store, and Laundromat.

She paid particular attention to the Laundromat when she saw a woman emerge with a large bright blue bag.

"That's Mrs. East, the minister's wife," said Tim.

"Yes. I know her," said Felicity. "But I'm more interested in the bag. I suppose the Laundromat sells them?"

"Sure," said Tim. "A lot of people use them. They take away their nice clean folded clothes and bring their dirty laundry in them. Like the one Ruth was using when J. G. saw her."

"*Very* convenient," said Felicity.

She must have seen Freddie's startled look. "I mean very convenient for the *real* thief. If he or she used one of those bags the way John Farrell suspected Ruth of doing."

"*That* jerk!" growled Freddie.

"Don't be *too* hard on him," said Felicity. "He was thinking along the right lines, but about the wrong person."

"That's J. G.!" said Tim. "He's *always* doing it."

"So I'm beginning to realize," said Felicity. "I'm hoping that the fingertip search will help to concentrate his mind on the hard facts."

"Huh!" grunted Freddie.

Tim was feeling just as doubtful, but kept quiet. He couldn't imagine *anything* capable of pinning J. G.'s mind down to hard facts. Not without him using them as launching pads into outer space, where sniffer dogs and their mysterious handlers roamed, and ten-dollar bills grew into hundreds at the blink of his brown left eye.

Felicity turned to the houses on the hill with their wooden steps.

Once again she murmured, ". . . very convenient,"—but this time with one extra word: "*Also* very convenient!" She folded the map carefully and put it in her case.

Then she became brisk.

"Time I was going back. But before I do, here's one more assignment. Freddie, do you think you can draw an accurate picture of Hippo? Full face, like for a missing-person notice?"

"Well, sure, but—"

"Color it if you have time. So long as it looks like you're making a determined search, not just fooling around."

"Do you want us to post it someplace?" asked Tim. "The church bulletin board or—?"

"No. I want you to take it around after lunch, door to door, and ask if anyone's seen it lately. Maybe lying around someplace, dumped in someone's garbage. Just this neighborhood. And let me know if you get any unusual reactions." She turned to go. "Report to me at four thirty. The fax should be in by then. Oh—and pay special attention to the folks living on the hill. Whoever lives there should have a pretty good overview of the comings and goings of strangers."

"Yeah. Like from the Farrell house!" Freddie chimed in. Felicity ignored this and went on:

"And if you see John Farrell before I do, tell him I suggest that the search squad concentrate on that side, too. Because—"

The church bell started striking twelve. "Good heavens! That time already! Elaine will be wondering where I've gotten to!"

" 'Because'—what, Felicity?" Tim called after her.

But she was already rounding the corner onto West Main.

22

Door-to-Door Inquiries

Tim and Freddie made a bad start that afternoon.

Old Mr. Pallance laughed outright.

"Green hippos! I've been accused of seeing pink elephants but never green hippos!"

Another old man, Mr. Grant, didn't laugh at all. He scowled at the picture and growled. Growled and snarled, "What is this? Have I seen *Donald Duck? Gitoutahere!*"

Freddie was hurt. He'd worked hard on that picture. He'd taken pains to give it the right shade of bright sickly green. He'd even struggled to give Hippo's face the exact expression. And now this old fossil didn't even recognize it *was* a hippo!

At the Rossi house nobody answered the doorbell at first. A baby was hollering somewhere inside. Young Rory Rossi. When Mrs. Rossi came with him in her arms, he was still crying.

"Teething," she explained.

The kid's wails did die down when he saw the bright-colored picture.

He made a grab at it. Freddie backed away just in time.

"At least *he* seemed to like your artwork," said Tim as they walked away.

"Yeah, but only to eat it," said Freddie. "I remember Robyn when she was that age!"

LOST
IN THIS NEIGHBORHOOD

HAVE <u>YOU</u> SEEN THIS ~~PERSON~~ CREATURE?

Anyway, Mrs. Rossi hadn't been able to help them. She'd been at the doctor's with Rory most of yesterday morning and certainly hadn't seen any sign of any green hippo. In fact, the only likely breakthrough seemed to come when they tried the minister's house.

"Why, yes!" said Mrs. East. "Of course I've seen it! But it isn't *lost*! It's right here. . . . Just a minute."

The boys frowned at each other, perplexed. Then Freddie seemed to make up his mind.

"The *minister*?" he hissed. He nodded toward the backpack hanging from a hat peg in the hall. "I *wondered* about that!"

"Yes." Mrs. East was on her way back. She was hugging something. "Here he is. He doesn't have a cute red cap anymore. He's a different color, too."

The boys gaped. It was Hippo, all right. Or Hippo's twin. But the color *was* different. Primrose yellow, not light green. And there was a saucer in place of the hat.

"It looks like someone's given him a new paint job," muttered Freddie. He looked as if he were inspecting a stolen car.

"Oh, no," said Mrs. East. "He's always been like this. They came in different colors. Didn't your mom get one, too, Tim? About three years ago, when we bought this?"

She brightened.

"But it's certainly been successful. This popcorn is definitely healthier than the usual kind. And Joe's very fussy about healthy living. Jogs every day, all weathers."

Freddie stiffened. "Yes. With that *backpack*!"

"Oh, that, yes," said Mrs. East. "He stuffs it with hymnbooks. It gives him a stiffer workout, he says. Some days, after he finds he's been putting on weight, he doubles the number of hymnbooks."

"Well he *could've* been the one who swiped Hippo!" Freddie protested after they'd left the East doorstep. "If his own Hippo broke down and he happened to notice yours."

"Somehow I don't think Felicity would buy that," said Tim. "I mean the guy's a *minister*! . . . Anyway, their Hippo doesn't look busted. A bit battered, maybe—"

"Suit yourself!" growled Freddie.

The fact that Mr. East was a minister didn't count for much with Freddie, Tim guessed. Just being someone in authority—minister, teacher, even a cop—didn't mean a person wasn't capable of committing a crime. After all, as J. G. kept reminding everybody, Freddie's own *father* had been convicted of a crime, hadn't he?

This put Tim in mind of the Farrell house. They'd given it a miss on their way from the Pallance house to Mrs. Rossi's. But now Tim was curious.

"Come on," he said. "Let's see if he's got the squad organized yet. I'm sure I heard Ruth's voice while we were talking to Mrs. Rossi."

"Huh! He's probably still waiting for the sniffer dog to be sent on loan from the FBI narcotics division," said Freddie. "Fat chance of *his*—"

Even before Freddie could complete the comment, they were both riveted by a sudden yapping coming from the top of the steps leading to the Farrell house. The door was wide open.

23

The World's Worst Sniffer Dog

"That sounds like it now!" said Tim, rather awed.

"Well, it's *a* dog, anyway!"

It was a beagle. Looking ready for anything, bright-eyed, with its tail up. Not so much wagging that tail as beckoning, seeming to say to someone behind, "Come on and *get* me then!" It was standing over something between its front paws. Then, as the yells behind it grew louder, it dipped its head to the article, gave it a joyously growling shake, and came out onto the steps.

"It's a sneaker!" said Tim.

"A red-and-white sneaker!" said Freddie. "Ruth's!"

The dog paused on the third or fourth step, turning to growl cheerful defiance at the kids who'd now reached the door. J. G. came first, looking pained, then Spencer Curtis, looking worried, then Ruth. She was hopping. Not just hopping mad, either. Her right foot was bare.

"It *is* Ruth's!" said Freddie, grabbing the dog's collar. "Come here, *you!*"

"Hold him," said J. G. coolly. "He's needed for the search."

"You mean *this—this—*is the *sniffer* dog?" jeered Freddie.

"Yeah!" said Spencer. "Sweets. That's his name. And he's not a *this*, thank you. He's a *he.* . . . Drop it, Sweets. You don't know where it's been."

Ruth snorted. "It's been on *my foot,* that's where it's been!"

J. G. had turned on Spencer. "I thought he was crazy over *popcorn*, not smelly old sneakers!"

Spencer flushed crimson. He was usually quiet and docile, but obviously not when anyone bad-mouthed his dog!

"He *is* crazy over popcorn!" he protested. "That's why we call him Sweets, stupid! Any kind of sweet stuff. This must be—"

Ruth's own indignation had melted away. "It's my fault, I hid a piece in my sneaker, didn't I, Sweets?" She patted the dog between the ears and he wagged both his tail and his tongue. The tail thrashed his owner's leg and the tongue licked Ruth's face.

"Get away from it!" said her brother. "You don't know where *it's* been!" He was feeling inside the sneaker. He looked puzzled. "There's no popcorn in here *now*."

Then Robyn, fresh on the scene, piped up.

"It dropped out in the hall when he rushed from the kitchen. Here, look. I picked it up."

Freddie took the piece from her. He suddenly frowned. "Hey! What *is* this?" he drawled. "It's the same kind as yours, Tim. The kind that Hippo makes!"

Tim stared.

"Yeah. It is. Exactly . . ."

"Of course it is!" said J. G. "There'd be no point in testing it with a *different* kind. Like this stuff—" he reached in his pocket and pulled out a crumpled sandwich bag with some sticky-looking brownish pieces inside—"that his handler brought along."

He glared at Spencer.

"But he usually goes for that kind, J. G.!" he said. "The sticky-sweet molasses kind."

J. G. shook his head slowly, snootily.

"But that doesn't happen to be the kind we're searching for—

dummy! That's why I just went to the trouble of making some of the dry, low-cal kind, for a *proper* test."

Freddie looked up sharply.

"Oh yeah? What did you make it with, J. G.? What kind of popper?"

Tim's heart gave a lurch. Was Freddie suspecting that Hippo was right *here* in the Farrell house?

J. G. sighed heavily.

"Come back here and I'll show you," he said, leading the way into the hall. "Mind the probing staffs!" He pointed down to the floor, near the wall. They looked like a bundle of old golf clubs, field hockey sticks, and various long thin poles, with a golf bag lying on top of them. "For probing the undergrowth with," he said.

Tim sighed. J. G. never did things by halves.

He'd certainly brought together a sizable squad. Holly Jenks and Julie Fisher were still in the kitchen, munching popcorn. There was a regular corn popper on the counter. Tim recognized it as the hot-air kind, with a yellow plastic base and a clear plastic chute. The bowl at the bottom of the chute still had a few pieces left.

"Hey! Quit eating the test material!" J. G. said to the two girls.

Tim bent closer to the bowl. The pieces were exactly the same as if Hippo had made them.

"You too, Tim!" said J.G. "Keep out of there!"

"Where are you going to test it?" asked Freddie, still looking disappointed at not finding Hippo there. "And when?"

"I just did!" said Ruth. "I hid a piece in my sneaker."

J. G. scowled. "Yeah! But that was jumping the gun. And you've seen what good *that* was! . . . *Now*," he continued, picking up the bowl, "we'll do this correctly. The mutt's going to be searching outside, right?" Sweets looked up at him and wagged his tail harder. "So outside is where we'll run the test. Spencer, keep hold of him in here while I arrange the test material out of his sight. He probably cheats like crazy!"

The rest of them followed J. G. out. He planted the few remaining popcorns singly here and there in the grass at the side of the steps. *"This'll* show if he's any good."

Freddie plucked Tim's sleeve. "You see what the jerk's doing, don't you?" he whispered.

"What?"

"Covering up the evidence!" whispered Freddie. "If he *is* the perpetrator and he dropped any of *your* popcorn out of Hippo there, while he checked the roll—well, it won't matter now. We'll never know for sure whether it was part of this test bunch or not."

"That's if the dog finds any at all!" Tim murmured.

For now Sweets was being brought out on a leash, tugging at it.

"Hold it tight!" said J. G. "And keep it short! We don't want him eating the evidence when we do it for real!"

"I know my job, thank you," said the handler. "What is it, boy?"

Sweets was now sniffing in the grass, his tail wagging furiously.

"He's found some already!" said J. G., looking triumphant as the dog suddenly stiffened, whimpering softly.

"Nargh!" said Spencer, keeping tight hold and pulling back on the dog's leash. "It's just a bunch of old dry leaves. . . ."

"It's one of my dad's old chewed-up cheroots," said J. G., sounding bitterly disappointed. "What's *with* the dog? I can see some of the popcorn *myself*, only inches away!"

"Come off it, boy!" said Spencer, yanking the dog's head away from the cheroot scraps. He glared at J. G. "Now it's ruined his smell for the rest of the day—well, for the next half hour at least. What d'you leave stinking old cheroots lying around there for? He'll never pass his test now! Now, if the popcorn had been the molasses kind, he'd have gone straight for them but—"

"Quit going on and *on* about the molasses kind!" snapped J. G. "Anyway, while we're waiting for his delicate nose to recover, we'll try out our special fingertip search frame."

He darted into the house and came out with a couple of canes from the bundle in the hall. There was some string wrapped around them. When he unrolled it and spread the contraption on the level grass at the top of the slope, it turned out to mark a three-foot-square patch, with the canes at either end and the string forming the other two sides. Like this:

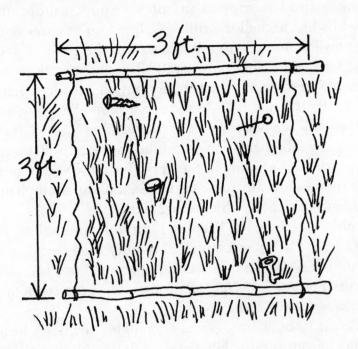

"That makes a nice convenient area to search for very small objects, square by square," said J. G. "Show them how it works, Julie, the way we planned. You too, Robyn. Go get your search gear."

While the girls ran back into the house, Freddie glowered, no doubt annoyed at the way his sisters were being bossed around by his archenemy, and Tim was thinking, Boy! What a team! The world's worst detective and the world's worst sniffer dog! With the youngest Fisher kids all bubbling excited like it was nothing more important than a Sunday school Easter egg treasure hunt!

He wondered if Felicity knew what she'd been doing, helping to set this up. It seemed to him to be a great recipe for total neighborhood disruption, mayhem, and disaster.

24

Sweets Makes a Very Important Find

The girls' "search gear" turned out to be a pair of black leather gloves for Julie and a pair of kneepads for Robyn. The gloves looked as if they'd been borrowed from Mrs. Farrell's cleaning materials. They were smeared with paint and polish and were about three sizes too big. The kneepads had a familiar appearance.

They looked as if they'd been ripped from somebody's football pants. Freddie hoped they were J. G.'s, not his.

Julie was complaining already about the gloves as she stood upside down in the trial square. "They keep slipping off! They'll upset my balance!"

"They'll protect your hands from any broken glass there might be down there," said J. G., "or rusty nails. So quit complaining. A good search squad leader always takes care of his crew!"

Then, after the two girls found a few small objects, like a penny green with mildew and a rusty stickpin, Holly Jenks sniffed, "I don't see why Julie Fisher should do the close searching standing on her hands, anyway. Showing off!" Holly was carrying a bunch of see-through sandwich bags as well as her notebook.

"With her eyes so close to the ground she can spot things other people might miss," said J. G.

"Me, too!" said Robyn. "I can't walk on my hands yet, but I'm little and my head is nearer the ground than other people's. 'Specially when I get on my hands and knees like this."

Julie said, "You look after your own stuff, Holly Jenks! Just be ready to make a note of whatever we turn up."

"Yeah! And bag it, don't forget!" said J. G. "Like I keep saying, we do this correctly or not at all!"

"Huh! *Correctly!*" squealed Holly as Sweets jumped up at the bunch of sandwich bags, sending some of them scattering.

"He thinks you've got some real molasses popcorn in there," said Spencer Curtis. "Come here, boy!"

After further squabbles, stumbles, and grumbles, J. G. picked up his special fingertip search frame, hitched the bag of assorted probing sticks onto his shoulder, and ordered the real search to begin down by the Kowalski house, at the spot that Felicity Snell had first suggested. Using the frame, he marked out the square partly over the short grass near the edge of the path and partly over the gravel, where Tim and Freddie had found the unpopped piece.

"He still thinks *I* was the thief, I bet!" growled Freddie.

Tim wished his friend would keep his voice down, but he needn't have worried, because just then Sweets and Spencer were creating a ruckus of their own.

The dog had pounced on a puddle in the road near the search square and was eagerly trying to slurp it up. Spencer yelled at him to get out of it, tugging at the leash. The leash got tangled in Julie's left hand, causing her to lose her balance completely as she collided with Robyn, knocking *her* over.

So what with Spencer's yells, Sweets's yelps, Julie's startled cries, Robyn's howls of protest, and J. G.'s angry commands, it looked as if Tim's prediction of disaster and neighborhood disruption was fast coming true.

"Argh! Let's get straight on to the *main* search!" said J. G. "See if you can do *that* right. Choose your own probing sticks. We'll see if the corn popper *itself* has been dumped nearby."

Swinging a golf club, he was leading the way to the tall grass and weeds bordering the road leading to West Main.

"There!" said Freddie. "He's keeping to the route Ruth took from your house to the Laundromat. He suspects *she* might have dumped it in those weeds after taking out the money!"

Ruth herself didn't seem to be worried as she slashed at the undergrowth with a field hockey stick. Neither did Julie, or Robyn, looking glad to be on their feet again, as they joined in the probing and prodding. And swinging. And slashing.

Soon more than one searcher was getting clipped with carelessly swinging golf clubs, hockey sticks, or other probing staffs. Cries of pain and anger, command and counter-command, rose in the air, destroying the peace of that normally quiet neighborhood. Not to mention yapping and barking.

"Ouch! That was my knee!"

"Well, look where you're going then!"

"Keep in line, shoulder to shoulder, then you *can't* get hurt. . . . And keep that dog from under our feet!"

"*You* try keeping him by your side when he's slipped his leash!"

"*You're* the dog handler, dummy, not me! And what did you let him slip his leash for, anyway?"

"Well, it's all the fuss and noise. *I* can't help it!"

"Ouch! *My* elbow!"

"That was my foot you just stomped!"

Then it happened. Holly Jenks raised the most piercing yell of all as Sweets, covered in pollen and seeds, came bounding out of the weeds and laid something at her feet.

Well, *on* her feet, actually . . . .

"*It's a dead rat!*" she screamed. And screamed and screamed and went on screaming, her twitching face turning purple with terror and outrage.

Sweets crouched, tail drooping, rolling his eyes and looking as surprised as anyone else. This was human gratitude for you! he seemed to be saying.

He'd seen Holly Jenks bagging various objects that Julie and Robyn had turned up in their trial close search. Dull, unexciting objects like a muddy nickel and a tarnished stickpin. Now he'd brought her *his* find—this juicy morsel, direct to her feet—and what did she do but holler and howl and kick the gift away! Just when he thought he'd be rewarded with some of that *real* popcorn, that sweet-sticky stuff. He knew there *was* some around. He could smell it even in the road.

"Giddouta here!" snarled J. G., looking as if he aimed to reward the animal with a kick himself.

"You leave that dog alone!" growled Spencer, brandishing his hockey stick.

And Holly's screams continued redoubled as she caught a glimpse of the dead rat's right eye staring beadily up at her as if it were all her fault.

In short, like everything else J. G. organized, all his elaborate plans and devices *were* ending in chaos. Just as Tim had foreseen.

"Mr. Farrell's going to just *love* this when he gets home!" Tim said, noting the worried faces that were now beginning to appear at doors and windows.

"Come on!" murmured Freddie. "I think that's his car on West Main, waiting to turn in. This is Mr. Know-it-all Ace Detective's problem, not ours! Let's me and you get on with our own investigating."

After that, their own luck wasn't much better.

There was nobody home at the Jones's house or the Dempseys'. There *was* someone in at Mrs. Peters's apartment, below the

Dempseys'. They even saw her through the living room window, sitting in front of the TV. But despite their ringing and knocking, the old lady went on staring at the screen.

"Big soap buff," Tim explained. "She wouldn't be able to give us any useful information, anyway. It's a wonder the thief didn't sneak in and swipe something of *hers*, as well."

"Maybe *she* keeps *her* door locked," murmured Freddie, trying the handle. "Yeah . . . see?"

Feeling dejected, Tim decided to give the Kilkinder house another try. They'd already been there and received no reply. But Tim had noticed Ms. Kilkinder's car parked in its usual space, and Freddie had sworn he'd seen a bedroom curtain twitch.

"Maybe she's just slipped out to the Laundromat," Tim had said. But Felicity *had* told them to pay special attention to the people living on the slope.

So once again they plodded up the twenty-one wooden steps and rang the bell.

No answer.

The car was still parked down below.

Tim looked up at the windows.

No movement.

"Maybe she can't hear for all the noise going on down there."

Freddie must have been mistaken about seeing Mr. Farrell's car. There had been a slight lull in the squabbling for a time, but now the noise level was mounting again. Tim could see the searchers gathering around J. G., and he wondered if Sweets had found another dead rat. The dog was certainly barking about something his handler had in his hand. J. G. himself had grabbed hold of the leash and was trying to pull the dog away.

Freddie pressed the bell once more, long and hard. Again no answer.

"Hmm, interesting . . . ," Freddie murmured as they went back down the steps.

"What is?"

"When I rang that second time, I definitely heard someone moving about, just the other side of the door. *Someone* was home."

Tim shrugged. "So what? She probably didn't think it was worth answering when she saw it was only a couple of kids. . . . Come on, Freddie. Forget it. It's time we were getting back to Felicity."

The church clock was just striking four thirty.

25

Spencer Demands an Autopsy

As they drew closer to the knot of kids, Tim saw that the object in Spencer's hands was a white mug, which he was trying to stuff into one of Holly Jenks's sandwich bags. The dead rat itself was already tucked away in another see-through bag on the ground at the edge of the road, well away from Holly Jenks. Holly still looked hot and flushed but seemed to have quieted down some. Even so, she kept casting anxious glances at the bagged rat and the mug that Spencer was trying to add to the collection of finds.

J. G. wasn't looking so pleased himself.

"Come on, come on!" he snapped at Spencer. "We're looking for the corn popper, not some grungy old chipped mug!"

"Nor dead rats, either!" added Holly.

"I know," said Spencer, at last getting the mug fully inside the bag. "But this could be rat poison inside it." He peered into the bag. "This brown stuff. It coulda been what the rat had ate!"

Tim and Freddie moved closer. Sure enough, there was an evil-looking brown liquid in the bottom of the mug. And there were dribbly brown stains up the side where it had been slopped around. It was chipped, as J. G. had said. It was smeared with mud on the outside and, like Sweets himself, it had bits of grass and seeds stuck to it in places.

"We need to keep it to show the veterinarian if *Sweets* is took ill, too!" said Spencer. "I demand a—a—one of those examinations to show the cause of death."

"An autopsy," said Ruth. "Yes! Felicity could handle *that*!"

This produced a burst of noisy gleeful agreement from most of the others.

"We found Sweets sniffing at it in there," Julie explained to Freddie, pointing to where the weeds were thickest.

"What?" asked Freddie. "The mug?"

"Yes," said Ruth. "Spencer had to work real hard, dragging him off it."

Tim looked at the dog. Sweets was very lively now, anyway— yapping and jumping up at the bag in Spencer's hands.

"That rat *wasn't* poisoned though, Spence," said Ruth. "It had a broken neck. Sweets himself might have killed it."

Holly Jenks shuddered. "Oh, no, he didn't! That rat was *stiff*. That's rigor whatsis." Her face was twitching again. "It had been dead for *hours*!"

"Some other dog could have done it, then," said Ruth. "And the word is rigor *mortis,* by the way. Stiffness caused by death."

Suddenly J. G. erupted.

"Autopsy? Rigor mortis? What *is* this? A murder mystery? *Who Killed Ricardo Rat?*"

"It was a field mouse, anyway!" said Ruth, picking up the other sandwich bag. "Look at that dear little face!"

"*You* look at it then!" said Holly, stumbling into J. G. in her haste to get away. "But don't bring it near *me*!"

J. G. gave her an impatient shove. "This isn't getting us any nearer to finding the popper. Now, get on the case! All of you!"

As Freddie and Tim began to move away, Freddie took a last hard look at the mug.

"Are you thinking what I'm thinking?" he murmured.

"I sure am," said Tim. "We'll report it to Felicity when we get to the library. See if she thinks so, too!"

26

Felicity Fingers a Suspect

When the boys arrived at the library, Felicity led them to a table.

"The case is beginning to break," she said, before they could give her their news.

"You've received the fax—?" Tim began.

"Yes. But first let's hear about the door-to-door inquiries."

She frowned at the report about the not-ins whom they suspected of really being in.

"You're sure about this Ms. Kilkinder?"

"Oh, yes," said Tim. "She must have seen us coming."

The visit to Mrs. Peters also interested Felicity. Especially when Tim made his comment about it being a wonder the sneak-thief hadn't struck at *her* house.

"But her door was locked," Freddie pointed out.

"How do you know?"

"I tried it."

Felicity looked up at him. "Hm! . . . I hope you did it discreetly. People can get the wrong idea when they see someone trying locked doors. . . ."

That silenced them both for the time being.

She moved on quickly to the next report.

"You say you got an unusual reaction from Mrs. East?"

"*Very!*" said Tim.

Felicity shook her head.

"I should have warned you. I've been making inquiries myself. Seems there was a big consignment of Hippos in town some years ago. Made in Taiwan. Various colors, same model. . . . So the Easts' Hippo is still in regular use?"

Tim told her of Mr. East's healthy eating habits. "Which reminded Freddie of the reverend's jogging and that backpack of his. And the opportunity Mr. East would have of sneaking in and smuggling out *our* Hippo."

"Plus the *motive*," added Freddie. "Especially if his own was busted."

"But of course Mr. East is a *minister*," said Tim. "And—"

"That shouldn't make any difference when you're investigating a crime," Felicity cut in. "Freddie was quite right to consider the possibility." Freddie's face glowed with pleasure. "But the main thing is actual concrete evidence. And the concrete evidence in this case is the footprints themselves. Prints made by jogging shoes *always* have a distinctive pattern. And our perpetrator wore a very different kind of footwear. *These* . . . ."

She plucked some sheets of paper from between the pages of the notepad.

"The fax results."

They stared at the first page. There were several lines of scribbled handwriting—presumably from someone at the Coast-to-Coast Investigations library. But Felicity was pointing to the bottom of the page. And there, staring right back at them, was this:

"What—what's *that* mean?" said Freddie.

"A play on the words, 'You beauties!' The second page, with some of the manufacturer's publicity spiel, explains everything," said Felicity, turning to it.

> Sheepskin slippers from Australia,
> made from the skin of ewe lambs.
> So soft, so gentle, so beautifully relaxing. . . .
> Baby your feet
> with ewe bootees!®
> As supplied to NASA for use by their astronauts
> Out of this world!
> "So snug you don't even know you're wearing them!"
> Col. Caroline Q. Rifkin, USAF

"So now we know we're looking for—" Felicity began checking the points off on her fingers—"*One*—a woman. This is definitely a woman's footwear."

She paused thoughtfully for a couple of seconds.

"Interestingly enough, it was John Farrell who first put me in mind of slippers. When he suggested Ruth could have worn some to disguise her footprints."

"The jerk!" said Freddie. "But you soon shot *that* down, Felicity."

"Yes. But sometimes people with wild screwball theories throw up some useful ideas. Never forget that! Anyway, here we have some concrete evidence that slippers *were* used. Not by Ruth, of course. But by the true perpetrator."

Felicity still had one finger stretched out. She now resumed her counting.

"*Two*—a housewife, or a woman who's home all day on sick leave. *Three*—a neighbor. Near enough not to bother putting anything more substantial on her feet. And *four*—a neighbor with a good view of your house."

The boys were silent.

They'd quite forgotten for the moment about the fingertip search and Sweets's find. But they soon remembered it when Felicity made her next remark!

"And that," said Felicity finally, "would account for the mug of sugar."

"Huh?" Then: "Hey, yeah!" they said together.

"A *very* neighborly thing. The neighbor who runs out of sugar and borrows some. Usually in a mug or cup. And not just with sugar. Only yesterday, Ms. Fitch in the reference library came down to return some tea bags she'd borrowed. Guess what she brought them in!"

"But no one's borrowed any sugar from us," said Tim. "Not lately."

"The sneak-thief didn't have to," said Felicity. "It was just a phantom clue. To fool any chance passerby. Something to make it look as if she was just an ordinary neighbor, slipping in and out of another neighbor's house to return something."

"Hey, yeah!" said Freddie once more. "And I bet she was toting another phantom clue. Something to conceal Hippo in that wouldn't arouse suspicion. Like the minister's backpack wouldn't have. I bet *she* had a Laundromat bag."

"So do I!" said Felicity. "That was another idea John Farrell put me in mind of."

The boys looked at each other. Tim himself was getting kind of tired of all this approval for J. G.'s lucky shots, and he was sure Freddie was feeling that way, too. So what about the major brownie points that J. G. would earn for his fingertip search when they told Felicity of Sweets's find? Even if J. G. himself hadn't realized the significance of the mug in his haste to get on with his search for the corn popper?

"There's something we have to tell you," said Tim, fighting down his jealous reluctance. "A new clue that's turned up this afternoon."

"Oh, yes?" said Felicity. "Where did you find it?"

"Uh—well," said Tim, "it's where Sweets found it really."

"Sweets?" Felicity looked puzzled.

"The—uh—sniffer dog," said Freddie.

"Spencer Curtis's actually," said Tim. He sighed. He wasn't finding it so easy, giving credit where it was due. "J. G.'s idea. For the Fingertip Search Squad."

"Go on," said Felicity, looking interested.

So they told her. About the dog's sweet tooth. About his indifference to the plain pieces of popcorn he was supposed to be looking for, and his preference for Spencer's molasses kind. About his not finding anything near the spot Felicity had suggested as the starting point. About J. G.'s losing patience. . . .

"Some detective that!" said Freddie. "Not having patience! Always pressing on! Always jumping the gun! Always—"

"Go on," said Felicity, not looking any too patient herself just then. "Then what?"

So Tim told her of the dead rat or field mouse and finally the finding of the mug.

Felicity slowly nodded. Her eyes had lit up, a bright violet, and now they were slightly narrowed.

"Yes," she said. "I'm sure you're right. That would be *the* mug. The perpetrator was beginning to find it was getting in her way. She must have found it an especial nuisance when she was checking on the roll she fished out at the end of your path. All fingers and thumbs in her impatience and eagerness. She probably spilled some more sugar there. Probably in the puddle Sweets found so attractive. You know—like some animals go for a salt lick. He must have thought he'd found a sugar lick!

"Then the perpetrator must have remembered spilling some in the kitchen. Maybe it would be better not to risk being seen carrying the rest of it around. It was, after all, no longer a phantom clue, but real evidence of being at the scene of a crime. So she decided to get rid of it at once. And what better way of dumping it than in the weeds right there across the road? Just an ordinary old beaten-up white mug—nobody would ever suspect whose it was."

"You keep referring to the thief as 'she,' Felicity," said Tim.

"Oh, yes. No doubt about it now in my mind!"

"Well," said Tim, deciding that J. G. shouldn't get *all* the brownie points, "I bet the person we're looking for is Ms. Kilkinder. She fits all these points. A woman. Home all day. A close neighbor. Good view of our house."

Felicity nodded. "Yes, the view. It's what I was saying earlier. Only *then* I was thinking about someone up there being able to spot any *strangers* looking for opportunities to steal."

"Yes, but—"

"But opportunist sneak-thieves come in two kinds," Felicity continued. "Those who go roaming around looking for opportunities. And those who stay in one place, *waiting* their chance. *Our* perpetrator is the second kind. And, like you, Tim, I'm beginning to believe that she lives right *here*."

Felicity tapped the map directly over the house with all the steps.

"But I still need a bit more information. So here's what I want you both to do. . . . Go back up there and try again. Don't worry if you still don't get a reply. What I want you to check is exactly how *good* a view she has." She turned to Tim. "What size TV screen do you use for your games?"

"Twenty-seven inch."

"Okay. So before you go up to her house this time, switch the set on, at the brightest setting. Then see how apparent it is from up there."

"We're on our way!" said Tim.

"Hey!" Felicity called after them. "And when you see John Farrell, be sure to remind him this time to concentrate the search near the houses on the hillside. Especially the scrubby patches on the high ground at the back of Ms. Kilkinder's."

Ten minutes later, they were climbing the Kilkinder steps again.

There was no sign of J. G. or any of the other searchers this time, but the two boys didn't go looking for them. They were in too big a hurry, eager to carry out Felicity's test.

Over at Tim's house, they'd lost no time in switching on the set. They hadn't even paused to pick up the card someone had dropped between the screen and the kitchen door. "Probably the Avon lady," Tim had muttered. "Come on. The car isn't there anymore."

Nobody answered their ring so they concentrated looking down at the window of Tim's room.

The result gladdened their hearts.

Whether from the front door or from any point on the deck in front of the Kilkinder house, the bright-colored flickering was visible.

"On a dull morning it would look even brighter," said Tim.

"Yeah! She'd even be able to see our heads in front of it!"

"That's good enough for me," said Tim. "Let's go switch it off before I forget. I wouldn't want Mom to come home and think we've been playing Power Patrol."

"This is a whole lot better than Power Patrol!" said his friend.

And that was really something, coming from Fast Freddie, king of the video arcade!

This time Tim did pick up the card.

"Hey, take a look at this!" he said. The printed inscription read:

Detective Richard V. Delaney

WEST MILBURY POLICE DEPARTMENT

Phone 555 2250

And on the back, scrawled in green ink, the words:

Stopped by 4:45 to investigate reported theft. Will call again tomorrow A.M. R.D.

"Must have been while we were at the library," said Tim.

"Yeah. We better call Felicity right away!"

All at once Freddie was looking very shaken.

27

The Most Important Victim Clue of All

"The sooner we wrap this up, the better!" said Felicity, when she heard the news over the phone.

Freddie breathed a great sigh of relief.

"So I'll be stopping by at your place straight after work, Tim," Felicity continued. "I need to ask your mom a few questions."

"Like what?"

"Like who might bear her a grudge. And who might have known about the stash. Then if Ms. Kilkinder fits, we'll have established a motive."

"Can't we just match her slippers with the footprints?" asked Tim.

Felicity laughed ruefully. "Not without a warrant! Only the police could order that. And we want to handle this without calling *them* in."

"Darned right we do!" Freddie blurted out, eyeing Detective Delaney's card, now pinned to the bulletin board.

Just then Felicity excused herself, explaining that John Farrell and the others were trooping in with a bunch of plastic bags.

"They look excited about something. Please hold while I see what they want. . . ."

They *sounded* excited, too, as Tim and Freddie listened at the other end.

The yapping of a dog came through loud and clear. So did Mr. Snerdoff's roar:

"No dogs in here, pilgrim!"

"I guess they've brought the mug," said Felicity, back on the phone to Tim and Freddie. "Also—ugh!—yes. The dead rat. . . . Not on the counter, Spencer, *please!*"

Then came Ruth's voice. "Spence is worried in case the brown stuff's rat poison."

Then Spencer's voice: "If Sweets has swallowed any, *he* might die, too!"

"I don't think so, Spencer," they heard Felicity say. "It smells . . . *mff! mff!*—yes—like brown sugar mixed with rainwater to me."

Then more barking, very close to the receiver this time, and Ernest Snerdoff's voice again: "If you don't take that mutt outa here right now, pilgrim, you'll really have something to worry about!"

After that, Felicity must have decided to hang up and concentrate on dealing with the developing situation under her nose. It was another hour before she arrived at Tim's house.

Mrs. Kowalski arrived at almost the same time as Felicity. She was very interested to hear about the Kilkinder possibility.

"*Does* she have a grudge against you?" asked Felicity. "Some neighbor feud? Some parking dispute, maybe?"

Mrs. Kowalski frowned. "Well, no. She leaves her car sprawled so that people can't get past easily when they want to turn at the circle. But *we've* never had a problem with it."

"Would you say she was a friendly person?"

"No, not really. A bit proud. You know—hoity-toity. Thinks she's better than the rest of us."

"Would you say she was the touchy kind?"

"Oh yes!" said Mrs. Kowalski. "Definitely. She hates to be

laughed at or have tricks played on her. There was a big ruckus last year over some trick-or-treaters. She even reported them to the police."

Felicity's face took on that sharp pouncing expression.

"Go on. Tell me more."

Freddie chipped in. "Yeah. Ruth was one of them. All they did was spray some shaving soap on her car. The cops didn't do anything." He grinned. "Ruth was going to take Mom's hair spray for the trick. As if *that* would have shown up! It was me who told her to use shaving foam."

"Hey!" said Mrs. Kowalski suddenly. "I just *remembered* a run-in we had with her. Something that happened at the salon. He just reminded me."

"Go on, Mrs. Kowalski!"

"Well, this was a few weeks ago. She'd come for her regular semi-permanent color and trim. Joanne, who was dealing with her, mixed her usual shade—Copper Gold. Unfortunately, the manufacturer must have mislabeled the bottle, and what *should* have been Copper Gold turned out to be Sunset Glow, which is more of a purply red."

"Oh, dear!" groaned Felicity.

"Yeah!" said Mrs. Kowalski. "It wasn't apparent while it was being mixed. But when Joanne had brushed it into the hair—Boy! It certainly showed up *then*!"

Mrs. Kowalski had to pause to control her voice.

"So what was Ms. Kilkinder's reaction?"

"Nearly hit the roof. Said it had all been done to spite her. Then Joanne burst into tears and I had to take over. Then the woman turned on *me* and said it was all *my* fault. She said I wasn't managing the place right!"

Mrs. Kowalski was looking mad. Trembling slightly.

"What did she mean by that, Mrs. Kowalski?"

"She—she said it was all the chattering and gossiping we did. It distracted the stylists' attention from what they were doing."

"*Had* there been a lot of—uh—gossiping?"

"Well, there usually *is*. You know. Nothing malicious. Nobody being hurt. In fact, some were telling stories against themselves."

"Like what?"

Felicity's nose was looking beaklike again.

"Like—" A curious expression was crossing Mrs. Kowalski's face. "Well, I'll be darned!"

"Go on."

"Well, you aren't going to believe this! But it was mostly about strange places where people stashed their backup housekeeping money. Someone said how they always used the refrigerator. Another said they used the deep freeze. Then it kind of escalated into tales of stashes hidden in coffee grinders, percolators, waffle irons, food mixers. You can imagine the accidents that have happened to rolls of greenbacks in places like that! And we were all laughing about it."

A faint smile was playing around Felicity's mouth.

"And did you happen to mention where you kept *your* stash?" she said.

Mrs. Kowalski glanced uneasily at the counter. "Well . . . as a rule I'd never mention anything like that. But . . ."

"But what, Mrs. Kowalski?"

"I was so busy trying to wash out the wrong color from Ms. Kilkinder's hair I wasn't thinking straight. I was concentrating on doing all the right customer relations things, too. Apologized. Told her there'd be no charge for this session. And—well—tried to keep up an interesting conversation to take her mind off the disaster."

"Including the corn popper stash?"

Mrs. Kowalski sighed. "Yes. I guess I did just touch on it. Saying I hoped I didn't forget and one day find Hippo spitting out popcorn gift-wrapped in dollar bills. You know. A little humor to ease a tricky situation. It worked, too. She even squeezed out a smile."

While his mother had been telling them all this, Tim had been thinking of Ernest Snerdoff and the red paint spill. Also of Felicity's theory about sudden emergencies loosening people's tongues. What a huge victim clue his mother had just admitted to letting slip!

"This happened a couple of weeks ago, you say?" murmured Felicity.

"Yes . . ."

"So obviously Ms. Kilkinder won't have forgotten?"

Tim's mother gave a bitter laugh.

"Probably remembers it every time she looks in the mirror! I tried with all kinds of colors, but it'll take a few more washings to really put that right. I notice she's taken to wearing a kind of bandana thing to cover it in the meantime. . . . So you think it might be her who stole the popper? Just to get back at me?"

"I'm pretty sure of it now," said Felicity. "And here's exactly what I think happened the other morning. . . ."

28

Felicity Reconstructs the Crime—and Confronts the Criminal

Felicity paused before continuing. Everyone waited in expectant silence.

Sounds of kids began to break in from somewhere outside. Excited, chattering, bickering sounds. Like a bunch of sparrows. Purposeless sounds—to anyone not in the know. But chock-full of purpose, really. Tim judged the noises to be coming from somewhere not too far away.

Like the higher ground at the back of the Kilkinder house.

Felicity seemed to be listening, too. A faint grim smile was beginning to play around her mouth. Then she resumed her account.

"First," said Felicity, "she sees you, Mrs. Kowalski, leave for work—and, a few minutes later, Freddie arrives. She then sees Tim's TV screen light up again. She knows how crazy these guys are over video games. She's probably heard you grumbling about it."

"Yes, I guess so," said Mrs. Kowalski, with a guilty sigh.

"So she realizes that this could be her big chance to get back at you. And what better way than to steal the stash she now knows all about?"

"Thanks to *you*, Mom!" Tim couldn't resist adding.

"But it's raining," said Felicity. "And she knows her cup of sugar trick won't look natural in that weather. So she watches out for a lull, getting more and more impatient."

"Yes," said Mrs. Kowalski. "Patience was never one of Selina Kilkinder's strong points."

"She does notice the boys break off, however," Felicity went on. "When they go down for a drink. And this reminds her she'll have to be quick if she ever does get the chance to slip into the kitchen.

"But then, when the rain stops and the sun comes out, she sees her chance. It's now or never. She sees the boys' heads still in front of the screen. She has the sugar and the laundry bag all ready to go. She doesn't bother to change into shoes. She'd probably forgotten she was wearing the slippers. As it said in that ad, they're 'so snug you don't even know you're wearing them.' So she slips across here. She's close enough now to hear the game noises—the shots, the screams, the screeching. Maybe even the players' comments."

"You *see*! I *told* you!" Mrs. Kowalski murmured at Tim.

"And then she tries the door," Felicity continued. "Knowing that not many people around here bother to lock up in broad daylight when they're still home."

"Especially kids!" said Tim's mother.

"Anyway, it *is* unlocked," said Felicity, "and she slips in. She doesn't waste time searching inside the popper. She just scoops the whole thing into the laundry bag and goes. All inside two minutes—tops."

Felicity then went on to mention how the woman had been too impatient and greedy to wait until she had got safely home before inspecting her haul. How she'd paused at the end of the path to give the roll of bills a rough check, spilling some more sugar; and how she'd thrown the mug into the weeds.

"The mean, horrible woman!" growled Mrs. Kowalski, thinking how long it had taken her to earn that money.

"And now she's just got back!" said Freddie, looking out of the window.

They heard the slam of a car door.

"Right!" said Felicity. "And this is where we confront her. . . . Freddie, Tim, have you still got your Missing Hippo notice? . . . Good! Bring it with you." She plucked Delaney's card from the bulletin board. "I'll take this—okay, Mrs. Kowalski?"

"Sure, but why don't I—?"

"No. You stay here. You're too emotionally involved and we need to keep cool heads. . . . Okay, you two. Let's go. But remember. Leave the talking to me."

Ms. Kilkinder's face reminded Tim of a snake's. Broad at the top, tapering smoothly to the chin, with two long, cold, almond-shaped eyes and a slitty mouth. It was so heavily made up it looked as if the skin had been given a thick coat of enamel. Today—as for the past weeks—it was topped off by the green-and-yellow bandana, twisted like a turban.

The masklike face didn't show much emotion. All that happened when she opened the door and saw Felicity and the boys was that the eyes became narrower, colder, harder.

The searchers' voices sounded louder from there. J. G.'s came through very clearly.

"I said, 'Shoulder to shoulder! Keep in line!' "

"We heard you!" Ruth's voice protested. "But how *can* we keep in line and shoulder to shoulder, with these bushes in the way?"

The cold eyes flickered uneasily, before turning back to the three visitors.

"Yes?" It came out as a snakelike hiss.

"We're wondering if you've seen anything of this?" said Felicity.

Freddie was holding up the Hippo notice.

146

The woman's eyes became even narrower.

"What is it? A toy or something?"

"Sort of," said Felicity. "The fact is, it's missing."

"Yeah!" Freddie murmured, before Felicity could check him. "From the Kowalski kitchen!"

He'd been looking at the woman's feet and seemed disappointed she wasn't wearing the slippers. In fact, she had on a pair of regular pumps.

She gave the kid a cold, baleful glance then turned to Felicity.

"So what? You're not accusing *me* of stealing it, are you?"

"Nobody said anything about that." Felicity kept her pleasant smile. "We're working on the theory that the thief might have dumped it in the vicinity." She gestured toward the sloping ground at the side of the steps. "In the bushes, maybe. Or under the steps. Or even in someone's garbage can. We were wondering if anyone might have seen—"

"*I* don't go around looking for discarded junk like some trashy corn popper."

"How did you know it was a corn popper, ma'am?" asked Felicity, her violet blue eyes staring into the woman's.

The cold eyes blinked. The tip of her tongue gave the thin lips a quick nervous lick. Felicity's question had certainly hit home.

"Well—uh—I recognize it now. . . . And anyway, you needn't look very far if it's sneak-thieves you're after." The cold eyes were now fixed on Freddie.

"Oh?" said Felicity.

Then the snake struck. "No! There are plenty people around here with a family history of thieving . . . . Like him, for one!"

"Me?" gasped Freddie.

"Yes!" hissed the woman. "Who else? Don't think I didn't see you this afternoon." She turned to Felicity. "Trying Mrs. Peters's door!"

Suddenly, Tim felt sick. It was like being back in the Pilgrim's Progress game again. They'd climbed what had seemed like the final ladder, but now they found themselves confronted by a very vicious, very cunning snake and seemed about to go falling right down to Square One.

But this time they had their Guardian Angel alongside.

Freddie was about to make an indignant retort, but Felicity beat him to it.

"There was a perfectly innocent reason for that, and I can vouch for it."

"Oh, yeah? And what does this have to do with you, anyway? I suppose those brats out back are with you as well?"

"I'm just trying to help recover the missing article," said Felicity. "I'm starting the junior library Mystery Club. I'm the new librarian there and this seems to be a very good exercise for them. And—"

"And I don't have to stand here answering your dumb questions!"

Felicity shrugged. "Suit yourself. Maybe you'd rather talk to Detective Delaney. He'll be stopping by tomorrow." She held out the detective's card.

The woman snatched at it, peered at it, shrank. After a moment's panic, she made a quick recovery.

"If he wants to ask me anything, he knows where I live. Not that I can help. Except to point out the suspicious way some people have been acting lately," she added, with another venomous look at Freddie.

She glanced at her watch, then up at the sky, now reddening in the afterglow of sundown.

Freddie's face was also burning. Before Felicity could stop him, he headed toward the garbage cans near the door.

"Mind if we take a look in here, ma'am?" he said, lifting the lid of the nearest one.

The woman quickly stepped forward and snatched the lid from him.

"You keep your hands out of there, Freddie Fisher! I don't want the place looking like a dump—like your own yard!"

Freddie turned to Felicity, but she'd frozen—gazing at the garbage cans with that ultra-violet look in her eyes. Then she snapped out of it.

She put two fingers to her mouth and produced a surprisingly piercing whistle, after which the sounds of the searchers suddenly ceased.

"Come on," she said to the boys. "That isn't any of our business. If the *police* wish to make a thorough search of the neighborhood, that's different. . . . Sorry to have bothered you, ma'am."

Ms. Kilkinder simply turned on her heel and slammed the door behind her.

"What was all that about the junior library Mystery Club, Felicity?" asked Tim as they went down the steps.

"Oh, it's something I really have been thinking about. In fact, I'm already arranging to have the use of that old, broken-down mobile library bus in the corner of the parking lot. When it's fixed up it'll make a great club headquarters."

"Like a police Incident Room?" said Freddie. "Like when they have a major crime to solve. Like murder. Like—"

"Yes. But right now we have to concentrate on *this* case and there isn't any time to lose. . . . Do you think your mother would mind, Tim, if I made a couple of urgent local phone calls?"

29

Felicity Goes Undercover Again

Selina Kilkinder didn't realize just how penetrating Felicity's observation could be. Even more penetrating than her whistle.

No. Those violet blue eyes didn't *really* have the power of X-rays. It was much more special than that. It was the power to pick up messages from the slightest of clues. And it was just such a message that Felicity had pieced together on that occasion.

Selina Kilkinder had, without opening her thin lips, told Felicity all she needed to know. Simply because of the various directions in which her eyes had turned. Such as:

1. The venomous look at Freddie when she heard that Detective Delaney was on the case.

2. The glance at her watch, and, immediately after that,

3. Her glance at the evening sky.

If Selina Kilkinder had sent the message by e-mail, it couldn't have been quicker or clearer to Felicity.

It said: *"I must get rid of the evidence as soon as possible. This very evening. After dark. Preferably in some place that will incriminate the Fisher kid."*

As Felicity explained later: "I don't think she'd gotten around to dumping Hippo in the undergrowth at all. I do think she'd stuffed it in the garbage can. When Freddie pulled off the lid, I noticed there was a kind of hole in the garbage. As if something bulky had been removed in a hurry, leaving the gap and causing some of the smaller items to be pulled out with it. Scraps of greasy foil and a couple of used tea bags still lying on the deck around the bottom of the can, as after a raccoon raid. She hadn't had time to clean them up. So I guess she'd been rattled by the sounds of the searchers closing in and had rescued the dumped popper before John Farrell and the others got around to finding it themselves. But now she was being forced to act fast. She couldn't risk leaving it in the kitchen with all this talk about a police search. So—'Where? Where?' she must have been asking herself. And ironically it was Freddie himself who suggested the ideal place by his interest in the garbage cans. That's when I decided to make those two phone calls."

The first was to tell Freddie's mother what was going on. How her son was in danger of being very callously framed. And what she, Felicity Snell, intended to do about it.

The second was to inform Detective Delaney that it was no longer a case of petty thieving. And that if he wanted to catch the real perpetrator he'd better drop everything he'd been planning to do that evening.

As a result, Detective Delaney put off a bowling date and the Fisher girls had the surprise of their lives. That was when their junior librarian visited them in their own home, just as darkness began to fall. She was accompanied by Tim, Freddie, and Mrs. Kowalski.

"What *is* this?" gasped Ruth, delighted. "A surprise party?"

"For *someone* it will be!" said Mrs. Fisher.

"Can we make it a barbecue party?" asked Ruth, beginning to dance with excitement.

"Out in the yard?" added Julie.

"With marshmallows?" Robyn chimed in. "And a campfire? And catching fireflies?"

"Later, maybe," said Felicity. "Some of that. Perhaps plus popcorn balls, which I'll show you how to make. But first we have to catch something bigger than a firefly."

"And in the meantime," Mrs. Fisher added, "*no one* goes out into the yard!"

"Except Felicity," said Freddie, frowning at the girls. "Got that?"

"Yes," said Felicity. "And I think it's time I moved into position."

She'd been looking out of the window. There wasn't much to see in the yard itself. The piles of leaf-filled garbage bags and the other junk were vague black shapes. But a car had just pulled up across the street a little farther along. Nobody got out. Someone inside lit a cigarette. Both Freddie and his mother stirred uneasily.

"Yes. It's Detective Delaney and his partner," said Felicity. "But don't worry. He's on your side this time, remember."

"Who? . . . Who? . . . Who's she talking about?" said the girls, as Felicity slipped out. "Who's she going to catch? . . . What? . . . A fox? . . . A raccoon? . . ."

"A hippopotamus if she's lucky!" said Tim.

"Anyway," said Mrs. Fisher, "if you want to watch, do it from your bedroom window. Only don't put the light on, and keep very quiet."

The window of the girls' bedroom was ideally placed. The light from the kitchen window was enough to make the dark shapes in the yard a little clearer. The watchers could see the glint of the light on the brass balls on an old bedpost and the softer reflections it made on some of the shiny black garbage bags. They could see the parked car and the cigarette glowing brighter from time to time. They could see the green flicker of fireflies dancing over the heap of rotting leaves that had spilled from a burst bag. But of Felicity herself—no sign.

"Where's she gone?" someone whispered.

"I don't know," murmured Mrs. Fisher. "Hush! I think someone's coming!"

The cigarette glow had suddenly been squashed out.

Then everyone held their breath, listening to the firm confident tapping of high heels as the dark figure of a woman rounded the corner of the street. Tall, thin, with a hood. . . .

No, correction, not a hood, thought Tim. Just a silk square, loosely draped over the head and tied under the chin. Tim recognized the colors, caught in the glow of the nearest streetlight. Green and yellow. The last time he'd seen them, the silk had been folded like a turban. Just to hide the hair, not the face.

Then something else caught his eye. Across the main street, opposite the intersection, four shadowy figures were clustered together under one of the big trees. He hadn't noticed them before, but now they were beginning to move into the street lighting. Three kids and one dog. The dog was having to be tugged away from the tree trunk. The kid in front, at the edge of the curb, tall and skinny, seemed impatient to cross, like he should have been on a leash himself. The second, a girl, was tugging at his belt. He turned and gesticulated impatiently at her and the kid with the dog.

Oh, no! thought Tim, quickly turning back to his observation of the woman. Fortunately, she didn't seem to have noticed the lurkers, and was now directly opposite the window he was looking through.

She had seemed to be hugging a large handbag under the arm nearer to the yard. But suddenly that arm jerked and the dark, bulky bag came sailing over the fence. It was all done in an instant. She hadn't even faltered in her pace.

But at that same instant, one of the black shapes in the yard came to life and leaped forward to grab the object that had just been tossed in.

"Got it, Rick!" Felicity's voice rang out.

And before the passerby could even turn her head, the car door opened and someone jumped out, shining a bright beam full on her.

"Police!" yelled the person with the flashlight. "Hold it, ma'am!"

It was a woman's voice, which for a second puzzled Tim, who'd been expecting Delaney.

Then a second person emerged and another flashlight beam lit up Felicity herself.

"Is it what you expected, Fliss?" said a man's voice.

"I think so, Rick." Felicity was untying the knot. "It isn't a Laundromat bag this time, but—yes!" She shone a small flashlight of her own into the garbage bag. "It's the corn popper, all right!"

Then she held it up.

And as she played the narrow beam on the grinning face of Hippo, with the green lights of fireflies dancing all around it, a great cheer went up from the hidden watchers.

A second, smaller cheer arose from the shadowy figures like an echo. They'd now made the crossing and were opposite the Fisher house themselves. This cheer was peppered by a joyous yapping.

"Nice work, Fliss!" said the man, stepping cautiously through the junk to join her.

"Thanks, Rick," said Felicity. "It's the first time I've gone undercover as a garbage bag! Oh—and please don't call me Fliss in front of the kids!"

But when they went indoors to get Mrs. Kowalski's and Tim's identification of the stolen article, while Delaney's partner was in the car with Selina Kilkinder, reading her her rights, the detective was as serious and formal as he'd been on that previous visit to the Fisher house, three years ago. He called Felicity "Ms. Snell" and even wrote Tim down in his notes as "Timothy Kowalski, son of the complainant."

Only for Freddie did he relax his official manner.

"Ms. Snell tells me that it was you who spotted the vital scrap of writing on the footprint," he said. And when Freddie said he guessed that was so, the cop's eyes smiled a little. "Nice work, kid," he murmured. "Maybe one day you'll think about becoming a detective yourself."

By this time, they'd been joined by the watchers from outside, who turned out to be J. G., Holly Jenks, and Spencer Curtis. Mrs. Fisher had invited them in, despite Detective Delaney's obvious disapproval of them. They'd kept quiet so far, even subdued in J. G.'s case, but now Delaney's commendation of Freddie's detective work proved way too much for The Kids' Own Detective.

"*I* helped too, sir!" he burst out (causing Sweets to break into a gruff bark that sounded eerily like "darned right!"). "Me and my Fingertip Search Squad! We spotted vital clues also!"

His right eye was gleaming at its silvery needle-sharp brightest—as if he'd been polishing it up especially for this occasion. Delaney wasn't one little bit impressed.

"*You* nearly blew everything!" he said sourly. "Following the suspect like that!"

"*Shadowing* her, sir," said J. G. "After we'd seen her sneaking away in the dark with the bag under her arm. That was careful scientifically-planned shad—"

"*Blundering!*" said the detective. "Getting in each others' way. *Arguing.* Even I could hear you from inside the car. Another minute and she'd have been spooked from carrying out her plan!"

"Don't be too hard on them, Rick," Felicity softly intervened. "They'd done some very valuable spooking work already. It's what made her act in such a hurry and give herself away, after all."

Delaney shrugged.

"If you say so, Fliss."

"I do say so, Rick."

The next morning Tim and Freddie went to the library to see if Felicity had any more news about the arrest and what Ms. Kilkinder had been charged with. She wasn't in the main building but Elaine soon directed them to the old mobile library in the parking lot. Felicity was already making arrangements for its new function as the Mystery Club's headquarters.

"Selina Kilkinder has been charged with attempting to prevent the course of justice," she told them. "But she's made a full confession, so I think she'll get off with a very severe warning. Plus she was smart enough to write out a check immediately to replace the stolen cash."

"That's a relief!" said Tim. "For the full two hundred and eighteen dollars, I hope?"

"That was the figure mentioned."

"Which now lets you completely off the hook, Tim," said Freddie. "Because we *know* Hippo won't have to be replaced."

"That's true," said Felicity. "There was nothing wrong with the popcorn he made last night in your kitchen."

It had certainly been the best popcorn Tim had ever tasted—after Felicity had coated it with hot molasses and sugar, then shaped it gently into balls, saying she'd learned to do it while working undercover as a short-order cook at Disneyland.

As if on cue at the mention of popcorn, there was a commotion at the door. J. G. with Holly and Spencer and Sweets had arrived. Before anyone could say anything, Sweets had slipped his leash and come bounding up to Felicity. The lady who'd made the chocolate *and* molasses popcorn balls was now his friend for life!

"This is great!" J. G. looked around at the empty shelves. "We can store clues on there, and here we can have maps and plans. You can be the official club artist, Freddie. And you can keep your case notes here, Holly—though I'd expect them to be up to date at all times, and a tad better spelled. And this . . ." His eyes lit up, both the gray and the brown, as he went to the driver's seat and perched himself on the backrest facing the others. "This is where I'll sit directing the planning and discussing and—"

"Just a second!" said Felicity. "What are you talking about?"

"The Mystery Club Special Investigation Unit," he said, with that superior smirk beginning to spread. He reached in his pocket and brought out the old pipe. Tim and Freddie gaped at him. He'd even come *prepared*! "With me as its director," he concluded.

"I think you're jumping the gun, aren't you, John?" said Felicity. "Mr. Hayes is kindly allowing us to use the van on one condition. That there'll be a member of staff in charge on all occasions."

"Oh sure!" said J. G., waving the pipe gently. "You'll be top brass, Felicity. The club's life president and like that. But operationally—"

"Operationally," said Felicity gently but very firmly, "I was thinking of splitting it into squads." J. G.'s face had fallen already, but it quickly brightened again as she continued. "Now *you* can be in charge of intensive investigations. The gathering of clues of every kind, masses and masses of them. So they grow and grow into a kind of giant snowball. A snowball that eventually catches up with the perpetrators and engulfs them Like an avalanche."

J. G.'s brown eye was glowing.

"Hey, yes! I like it, I like it! We could call it—uh—code name Snowball Squad!"

Then Freddie found his voice.

"Better yet. Why not code name *Screwball* Squad?"

J. G.'s brown eye didn't even flicker. But Felicity stepped in diplomatically all the same.

"Why not?" she said. "We had one called just that at Coast-to-Coast Investigations. The best brainstorming unit in the business. So don't you knock it, Freddie Fisher!"